I0782104

LIFE of PIES

SPECIAL COOKBOOK COLLECTOR EDITION

C. S. Johnson & Crystal McGough

Hardback ISBN: 978-1-948464-99-4

Ebook ISBN: 978-1-948464-80-2

HUMBLE PIE

A PRODIGAL SON RETURNS HOME

Life of Pies, #1

C. S. Johnson

CHAPTER ONE

Matthias "MD" Davidson

My palms are sweaty and hot against the fraying faux leather of my steering wheel as I drive. The road I'm on is dotted with potholes and lined with trees just starting to bloom after a hard, southern winter, but I only stare straight ahead, keeping my eyes forward as I lose my mind. I prefer to ignore the world, if I can. My soul festers and bleeds as the world is waking up with renewed hope, and I hate it for its disdainful apathy.

I don't want to do this.

My foot eases off the gas a little and I coast along on the highway.

I don't want to be here.

As much as I love Marjorie—my name for my beat up, old '98 Toyota Camry—I secretly begin to hope she'll break down and give me a divine exit to this last resort.

Hell, at this rate, I'd even settle for an abrupt exit.

Dying physically seems a lot easier than pretending to live, and that's what I'd been doing for the last nine months.

An exit sign along the interstate winks at me in the late morning sunshine.

It's the exit I'm looking for as much as the one I want to run from.

Now my hands are sweaty, hot, *and* shaking.

My heart is a lump in my throat, choking me more with every mile.

I swerve off the interstate, leaning into the curve of the road.

The road becomes increasingly cracked by erosion and I wish once more for some random semi to burst out of nowhere and slam right into me.

At twenty-eight years old, I'm still young enough to be fit without much work; I'd likely survive the crash.

But then I'd probably die waiting for an ambulance out here in nowheres-neck-of-the-woods.

I'm driving down from Nashville, one of the most constantly-surveilled cities in America. With every mile, I was leaving technology, civilization, and urban life farther behind, heading for my hometown of Fairmont, Alabama, a small town that might as well be a living time capsule reservation for twentieth century America.

I'm probably going to die anyway.

That's why I'm going home, after all.

I glance over at my cell phone, making sure it's off for the hundredth time since getting in the car this morning.

I am driving away from civilization and my dream life, but also from the several people I owe money to, ranging from my gullible best friend Dezmo, to the five or six relentless payday loan sharks eager to spill my blood into financial waters.

Maybe it wouldn't be the worst thing if I died …

I wouldn't have to worry about paying back the collective five hundred thousand dollars I owed to various lenders, and I'm even wearing clean underwear to boot, so Mama won't be completely embarrassed at my death. She'll only be upset I don't make it all the way home to see her again.

That's assuming she'll be happy at all. I don't really know how Mama feels about me coming, no matter how she sounded over the phone.

Calling her this morning had been the first time I'd talked to her in twelve years.

At that thought, I think about flooring Marjorie into the nearest telephone pole. My foot presses back down on the gas pedal semi-subconsciously.

That's when I see it: my hometown's welcome sign.

The sign welcoming travelers is a bright, colorful, newly-restored sign with "WELCOME TO FAIRMONT" spelled out in large, blue lettering. Underneath that line, the epigraph *"Home of Orpah Abraham, Alabama's Pie Queen and Legendary Daytime Star"* is written out in thick, yellow block letters, next to a cartoonish face of a proud, black woman with big hair, red lips, and a white smile with a gap in between the front teeth—Orpah Abraham herself.

It's too distracting for me to properly ram into it.

I can only stare, wondrously abhorred and jarred by its tackiness. The sign is so loud and new, it belongs in Vegas more than the slums of Fairmont.

It's all wrong—for the town, for the people here. And even for me, too.

It's true that Orpah's a big daytime television star. Ever since her failed run into politics a few years ago, she's been the host of "Be the Change," a morning news and entertainment program that Fairmont airs locally. The show occasionally travels throughout the northern Alabama area, and for her work, Orpah's been nominated for some Emmys, talked with several Hollywood elites, and cooked with the best Southern Belles. Generally, no one is outright willing to say anything bad about her.

And personally, I know firsthand that's all you can really hope for with a career in the spotlight.

But as good as she is on screen, I know for a fact Mama's pies are better than hers. I don't even have to taste test them to know.

Mama had grown up in Fairmont and gone off to cooking schools around the world. She eventually came back home to savor her roots, or so she'd said, and then she'd started her own catering business before our family fell apart.

That was when Papa left.

I frown at his memory. I hadn't seen him since Samantha was born, and she's nearly twelve now.

At least, I think she's close to twelve … okay, maybe she's fifteen. Does it matter? She probably still acts like a baby …

I grimace at the thought of my sister.

But my mouth waters at the memory of Mama's home cooking, and all of a sudden, I'm okay with not killing myself.

For now.

Swallowing hard, I pull the car into my mama's neighborhood.

Fairmont's always been a relatively small place. The houses I pass are varied in their designs, many with carports and wire fences. Some have unpaved driveways, a few have the old rabbit ears for getting cable over the airways—something I shudder to think of trying in my apartment condo back outside of Nashville.

The neighborhood here is clearly poor, but there's an almost noble quality to it, especially when I think of Nashville's neglected poor. Here, house after house is slowing rotting away, with small fixes ranging from broken shutters, unkempt lawns, and muddy driveways; some are clearly already worth demolishing and starting all over, with their smashed-in windows, holed-out roofs, and junked up front yards straight out of *Hoarders Non-Anonymous*.

Even after years of the city streets, the shady alleyways and the dilapidated hovels that the homeless make, it's surprising to see how poor the place looks.

It's even more surprising to see the bright, sunny yellow Beemer in Mama's driveway.

That's not Mama's car … is it? Surely, she wouldn't buy one.

I grit my teeth.

I remember how Mama struggled to make ends meet after Papa left. With me and my brother Asher, and then Samantha to care for, there were a few weeks we didn't eat much, and sometimes we would go days without food. We'd've starved if not for the food pantry at the Presbyterian church. As much as they helped us, Mama hated going to them, because they always wanted her to come to church and she often had to work or was too tired to go after working.

When I turned fourteen, I went to work to help out, and Asher followed after me a year later.

I frown, suddenly wondering where my brother is. Last I heard from him, he'd gone to community college and tried to start his own business. He'd called me up out of nowhere on my job line. Scared the hell out of me, too, but after he asked me for money and a visit, it was easier to cut him out of my life, too.

Especially since he knew about Mama's stash.

My jaw begins to tighten, and a moment later I have a cramp in my neck.

TMJD sucks.

I try to breathe, and then a moment passes, and I do my best to shrug it off.

Doesn't matter now …

I turn off Marjorie's engine, and the car happily goes off to sleep. I pat her wheel with my still-sweaty hand. "Good girl," I whisper, as I look up to my old house.

It's a small double-wide with a decent, if old, paint job. The windows are all shut and the vertical blinds are all lowered, save the one by the kitchen. Through the small

opening, the shadow of my mama whisks back and forth. I hope she's preparing lunch, but she could just as easily be pacing back and forth, wondering what she's gotten herself into by agreeing I could come home.

"Get some rest, Marj. I dunno how long I'm gonna be here. Maybe this is all for nothing."

Taking a deep breath, I open my car door and get out. My legs are a little like jelly, and while I'm hungry, especially for my mama's cooking, I feel too nervous to eat.

"Matthias? Is that you, honey?"

I nearly jump at hearing my name. My body is still tense as I turn around. It's not my mother, but it might as well be.

Standing on the porch next door is Edith Hennessey.

I force myself to smile as I hold up my hand in an awkward wave.

"Hi there, Mrs. Hennessey," I call back. "How are you this morning, ma'am?"

"It's just after noon now," Edith replies with a friendly smile. "But the day's been just lovely, and sure to be even better once the festival begins in a couple hours."

"Festival?"

"The Fairmont Spring Festival, of course. It's my Donnie's favorite time of the year, and plenty of others', too. You haven't forgotten us completely while you were away in your big fancy high-rise, did you?"

"Oh, right, the pie festival," I murmur. "No, ma'am, I haven't forgotten."

I'm lying, and Edith probably knows I am. But she probably doesn't care, either. I still live in the South, and I know how the South works. Lying is a forgivable offense, especially when it's done to show good manners or other virtues.

"Martha's always told me you were a good son," Edith says as she nods approvingly. "She tells me and Clarice about you and your brother at our Sunday brunches. Are you excited to see him? He should be here in a little while, I imagine."

"Of course." I can feel my smile fade; I didn't know my brother was coming home. "I'm sure Mama wanted everyone to be home."

I move closer to the front door, eager to leave this conversation.

Edith's a nice, older white lady, but not old-old, probably in her late forties or early fifties. She never had any children, but she still dresses in a modest, house-wife way. She even has a small string of pearls around her neck today.

In all my years away, she hasn't changed much. She's probably still married to her husband, Donnie, a veteran with PTSD and a bad temperament. He was never very nice, to her or others, and I remember wondering as a kid why she never left him. But then, she's one of the members of the Presbyterian church—or at least, she had been, back before I left.

Church folks live in their own world, and I preferred mine to theirs.

Usually.

I grimace at the thought of all the calls I've missed from Dez and others in the last few days.

"You might want to wait a moment," Edith calls out as she pulls out a cigarette and lights it. "Orpah's still in there."

"Orpah?" I recall the cartoon sign I passed. "Orpah Abraham?"

"The one and only," Edith says with a sneer. "She must've heard you were coming home and wanted your mama to come on her show. Ratings are down, but a star like you might turn things 'round."

"I doubt that; I'm not that interesting," I mutter. "But that explains the Beemer."

"Sure does." Edith snorts with a small laugh. "Don't worry, your mama will throw Miss Orpah out soon enough. Orpah's a pushy thing, but Martha and I both can't stand her. She'll say 'no,' and a hundred times later, Orpah will leave."

"Maybe she'll leave when they see I'm here," I say, opting for a quick exit to the conversation. I didn't ask for it, and I'm more than happy to get out of it.

"Well, go on then." Edith seems to catch on this time, and waves goodbye to me accordingly. "And good luck."

I nod and give her a nicer smile, trying not to grimace.

Good luck would be a nice change.

"Edith? Where are you?" Donnie Hennessey's voice comes hollering out of their house, and Edith lets out a disgruntled groan.

"Good luck to you, too, ma'am," I say.

From her grimace, I can tell it'd be a nice change for her, too.

Edith heads back into the house, her cigarette giving off a smoky trail behind her.

I make my way to the front door. It's open, but the screen door is still closed.

Realizing Mama could've heard me already, I straighten my shoulders, hold my head up high, check to make sure my collar is down, and smooth the wrinkles out of my shirt. I pat my hair down. My patch of bleach-blond hair is sweaty, too; it doesn't matter if it's only springtime in the South.

That's not the only place I'm sweating, either. I miss my days stuck working inside air-conditioned offices, radio stations, and night clubs.

I'm about to go in when I hear the voices.

"I've already told you, we've nothing more to talk about, Orpah."

Mama's frustrated.

It doesn't matter if it's been a dozen years since I'd been in her company; I can still hear her seething tone as she hides it under a polite veneer.

I don't know if it's good or not. Perhaps she'll be happier to see me by comparison now … or maybe she'll be more passive-aggressive because her nerves are already ruffled. But then, she probably doesn't know I'm here at all, and that's good news for me.

"What do you mean, 'nothing more to talk about,' Martha?" Orpah's voice is laced with anger. "This is utterly unacceptable."

"Unacceptable to you," Mama retorted.

"You did this to me on purpose!"

"As I recall, that's not what I said twelve years ago."

"How dare you!" Orpah huffs and hisses at the same time, and that makes the little boy in the back of my mind flinch in horror. "You're wrong about this, and you will regret this."

"I've already had my regrets, thank you kindly. But now I've made peace with the past, and you will be able to do that, too—one day, I hope."

There is a long, heavy silence, and then Mama speaks again. "My son'll be here soon, and I'd like to have everything perfect for him when he arrives."

There's a bit of a shuffling noise, and the oven squeaks open, and the sweet aroma of home comes rushing out.

I can smell it from here, and my eyes water as much as my mouth.

Pecan pie. Mama made me pecan pie.

I barely hear Orpah biting out her goodbyes.

A second later, Orpah's right there in front of me, even though she doesn't see me until she steps out of the house. Immediately, her eyes narrow but her smile widens. It's too much like Fairmont's welcome sign, and it's big enough I can see the gap between her two front teeth.

For some reason, it reminds me of a mask, and I realize the sentiment behind her smile is similar to how I just smiled at Edith.

"Well, Matteo, it's lovely to meet you at last!"

"It's Matthias, but—"

She doesn't hear me; instead, Orpah's arms open wide to grip me in a big, mama-bear hug. Squelched against her large bosom, I can smell her perfume, Chanel No. 5, and it clearly clashes with the rest of her personality. "I'm Orpah Abraham, but you're a smart boy, so I'm sure you've figured that out already."

I feel like she's testing me on some level, and she probably is. "Um, yes."

"See, you're so smart!" As she pulls away from me, Orpah is as bright and bubbly as she is polished and proud. She's wearing a bright red bauble necklace and a black lace top over golden silk, almost as if she's matching her Beemer. She's chatting amicably with me out of habit. Her eyeliner is thick and straight, and her cheeks have too much blush. Her red-painted lips move fast, flickering in between her pristine-white teeth.

"Your mama has been waiting for you for so long, Matteo," she rambles on. "So, you're enjoying your time in Nashville, I hear. You've gotten quite the reputation as a doctor."

"It's Matthias," I murmur. "And I'm not a doctor."

"But I heard you were an 'MD.'" Her tone goes dark and dramatic as a fake frown crinkles her face, and I feel the heat burn into my cheeks at the mention of my street name.

"Well, we all make mistakes," I say instead. "It was nice to see you, ma'am, but I'm sure you have other things to do with the festival. You're the Pie Queen, after all, aren't you?"

"Oh, yes. Yes, I am. Pardon me." She clucks her tongue and shakes her head. "I was just checking on your poor, old mother. She's had some health issues so I'm sure she's happy to see you before it gets worse."

"What do you mean?" I ask.

"It's just so sad, my dear," Orpah says, patting my arm in comfort. "She's been losing it lately. Making up all kinds of stories for money, or to reassure herself she's not a victim, thanks to your father."

I frown. "What do you know—"

"Oh, everyone knows your father left her because she was … well, never mind," Orpah says. "Excuse me. I'll let you spend the time with her yourself, and you'll likely see what I mean. My advice, should you want it, is that you shouldn't listen to anything she says, especially about your father or Samantha. But I know it's not my place to say such things, either."

There's a beeping noise from inside, and Mama appears at the window. "Matthias," she calls, waving me in before she goes and turns off the stove.

Orpah tugs on my sleeve. "I'm worried for her," she says in her dark, serious tone. "She hasn't been in a good place of late. Her mind is going, Matteo. Please promise me you'll let me know if she needs anything, alright?"

"Alright, ma'am."

I don't like how Orpah talks about my mama, especially since Orpah can't seem to remember my name. But what did I know? Orpah at least seems like she's been in my mother's life more than I had in the last twelve years.

The Beemer honks loudly as Orpah speeds off, and I am happy to see her go. She makes me uneasy. I don't know why she'd argue with Mama, but I also don't think she'd randomly tell me Mama's had some health problems for no good reason.

"Well, Matthias, you coming in or not, baby?"

I turn around to see Mama behind the screen door. Just like Edith, she's very much the same woman I remember, just a little more tired and a little more worn. Her skin is like weathered porcelain, much the same as my own; her hair, once a vibrant brown, has been dulled down with gray and white strands. Her eyes are still the same shade of sky blue, but more peaceful, now. Through the screen, I can see the wrinkles creasing through her brow as she scowls at the back of Orpah's Beemer.

"I'm glad she didn't scare you away." Mama's nose wrinkles disapprovingly. "I shouldn't have let her inside, but she's very convincing."

"She would have to be." My voice seems thick as I try to make small talk. "She's in television."

"Yes, and she's been in it too long, if you ask me." Mama opens the door for me, and I see she's wearing oven mitts. "Come in, baby. I made a special lunch for you."

"And Asher, too?" I ask, only a little accusingly as I look around the house.

"He'll be in around dinner, so this lunch is all for you."

Mama has a magical way of reassuring me, and it's even more potent as I step inside.

"Where's Samantha?"

"She wanted to go out and be on her own for a little while, so I let her."

"Is she able to do that?"

Mama arches an eyebrow at me. "Your sister is more than capable of being on her own. Otherwise, why would I've let her leave? I may not have been the best mother, but none of my children are in jail."

Yet.

I feel uneasy all of a sudden. I don't know if she knows about the trouble I'm in.

Before I can get too skeptical, she takes me by the arm and hugs me.

I don't have time to say no.

Her embrace is as quick as it is sure. Orpah's hug was practiced and measured— nothing like my mama's. As we stand there, I know without a doubt she still loves me.

She still smells like she's always smelled, like a faint bit of flowers and soap. Her hug is warm and loving and true, and all at once I want to lose myself in her hug like I'd done as a child.

Nothing has changed that over the years, even if everything else has changed.

I don't deserve this.

Again, I wonder if Mama knows how repulsive I've become as she finally pulls back.

"Well, let's eat," she says, drawing me over to the small dining room table.

It's full of all my former favorites—fried okra, collard greens, yams and southern pot roast. There's some homemade rolls in a small bread basket, and a small tray full of butter that's placed next to a gravy boat.

Mama sits down and loads up a plate with everything on it while my stomach does a backflip. Somewhere in the back of my mind, the latest keto-paleo-kale-happy diet plan is chiding me for even looking at the display before me, and as she drips gravy over everything, my body screams like a preacher catching me with porn.

My job in Nashville is full of trouble, obviously, but no one's going to respect me if I'm fat. No one's going to believe I can outrun any cops if I'm not in shape, either.

When Mama hands me the plate, I hesitate. "I'll get one for myself," I tell her.

"Don't tell me you're on some Yankee diet now," Mama says, but she dutifully puts the plate down in front of herself.

"No," I lie, before helping myself to the pot roast. I can see the bacon bits garnished over the turkey, but I ignore them as I scoop it onto my plate. I ignore the gravy and leave the cornbread and rolls and yams behind.

Mama frowns at me, but she says nothing.

Saying nothing is not nothing in the South, but I'll let it go until she breaks.

I eat and eat and Mama makes the usual chit-chat, telling me about Fairmont, and who's died, and who's moved, and who's married. She mentions a few names I know, but mostly I nod along just the same. I only really react when she mentions Asher.

"Are you excited about meeting Pamela?"

From the way she says it, I know I'm supposed to know who that is. But I don't. So I only shrug.

"Ash's very excited about her," Mama continues. "I'm certain he's bringing her here to meet us before they marry."

"He's proposed?" I scoop another stack of vegetables into my mouth. I wish I could use the gravy for this, but I know I can't.

I'm comforted by the smell of the pecan pie; I can skip the gravy. Otherwise, I'll have no room for dessert.

And for me, when it comes to desserts, pecan pie takes the cake.

"Oh, I doubt it. I told him if he wanted your grandmother's old ring, he could have it, and he said he'd like that."

"He always was your favorite," I retort, and Mama looks hurt by my accusation.

"I didn't mean it like that," she says. "I just figured if Ash was ready for marriage, he should have it. That's how your father got it. He popped the question to me nearly forty years ago now."

She looks down at her left hand, which has been left unadorned. "It would be nice for the ring to have a new home."

"If you say so."

She puts her hand on my arm. "Your father was a good man. We didn't always see eye to eye, and I'm sorry you had to grow up without him."

"I know Papa left and he had his reasons. It's pretty clear to me what happened now. But I didn't really want to talk about this," I murmur.

Mama's lips flatten. "I see." Her tone is tight and tense. "Perhaps we could talk about it anyway? Unless you have something you would like to tell me that's more important?"

"Maybe," I murmur, already feeling the heat from my cheeks.

"Well, *maybe* you'd like to tell me who this Dezmo character is who keeps calling me? And why I've been contacted by three different loan companies in the last couple of weeks?"

I say nothing. I put my fork down, wondering why I'd ever decided to come home.

"If you need money, it's no problem, Matthias."

"It's a lot of money."

Mama wrinkles her nose again. "I figured that much out on my own, son."

"To be fair, I know you have it." I finally look back up at her, meeting her gaze with mine. "You've had it since Papa left."

She stands up and takes her plate to the sink in silence. "I'll get some pie for you, baby," she says. "I know pecan's your favorite."

"Thanks."

She brings over the plate and sets it down in front of me. She has one for herself, too, but she's not eating.

I'm not, either.

Together, we just kind of stare down at the pie and each other, and a long while seems to pass before Mama clears her throat.

"I'm sorry about the past," she says. "I can't change it. And some of it, as painful as it was, I wouldn't change."

"Like what?" I ask, bitter all of a sudden.

"I wouldn't change Asher, or Samantha, or you, either. You're my son, and I love you."

"You didn't love Pops, though."

"I did. But love's not always enough, Matthias. I understand this now." She sighs as she stands up. She picks up her plate, the perfect slice of pecan pie still placed in the middle, and heads over to the oven. "Which is why I'll give you the money."

"You will?" I look up at her, full of both amazement and skepticism. "Why now?"

"I won't ask you for details why you need the money," Mama murmurs lightly. "And I'll ask you to give me the same treatment. That money was given to me under circumstances too horrid to speak of, and I'd rather not give it power over you—or others in our family."

She looks up toward the bedrooms, and for the first time, I hear a small shuffling noise.

Is there someone else here?

I'm distracted only briefly, before Mama hands me a check.

"Is this enough?" she asks, handing me a check for six hundred and five thousand, three hundred and eighty-four dollars and sixty-three cents. "That's all of it I've gotten over the years, including the interest."

My mouth drops open. I'm shocked and appalled, but also deeply grateful and profoundly moved by my mother's generosity.

The last time I'd asked about this money, all she said was it wasn't hers to give, and the devil would have her soul if she did.

I know suddenly, in looking at the check, that Mama is truly happy to see me, and enough so she's giving me—her wayward, stubborn, hardhearted son— something she's kept to herself for over a decade.

I run the check between my fingers, still astonished. Then I think of what Orpah told me on her way out.

"Are you feeling alright, Mama?" I ask.

She bristles at my question, but I can see her hands are shaking as she begins to clean up the meal she made for me.

"Please tell me if something's wrong," I press.

She shakes her head.

"How do I know this check won't bounce?" I ask, and she finally responds to my goading.

"It won't," Mama says. "You can check my account yourself, if you'd like. Garland Morris has been the bank teller here since before you were born, and he'll be able to tell you if it'll bounce or not."

"Okay," I agree. "But you would tell me if something was wrong, wouldn't you?"

"Honestly, Matthias, I don't know," Mama says slowly. "I am your mother, and I love you. I only want to protect you. And I don't think you can handle the truth very well."

"But I mean, like your health is okay, right?" I see her now, and I watch as her face turns green. Her hands are no longer shaking; they go limp as she clutches at her stomach.

She shakes her head, and suddenly, I'm more worried than I've ever been in all my life, including this morning.

"Mama!"

She falls away into a faint.

The check falls from my hands. I rush to catch her. I'm too late, and I hear the sickening *crunch* of her skull as she crashes onto the floor and begins to bleed. The pecan pie falls to the floor around her, and tears are flooding my vision as I try to get her to wake up.

"Mama?"

I barely realize that my younger sister, Samantha, is suddenly in the kitchen with me. She's holding the phone and pressing in the numbers for 9-1-1 as we both sit there, waiting and wailing as Mama doesn't wake up.

Did I do this? The question rings around in my head over and over again, and I don't have any answer.

Did she have a heart attack, learning I was desperately in debt and dealing in drugs?

Was it something I did?

Was it because I'd come home?

Did the devil really come for her soul as she gave me the check?

I just don't know; I don't have any answers. I hold her still-bleeding head in my lap, running my hands over her wrinkled cheeks.

I press a kiss on her cheek. "Oh, Mama," I whisper, more traumatized than ever when she stops breathing.

I'm not ready to say I love her. But I'm not ready to say goodbye, either.

"Pip," Samantha says, making me look up. She's on the phone. I'm not sure who she's talking to, but after a few emotional garbles that sound alien to me, she nods and says thank you, and I hear a semi-familiar voice that makes me cringe, telling Samantha that he's on his way over.

Before I can say anything—before I can get my mouth to properly form words again—Samantha's dialing a new number as she anxiously twists a lock of her black curls in her free hand.

"Asher?" Samantha's calling our brother. He hasn't picked up his phone, and she's leaving him a message. "Asher, where are you? You need to get here, now. Mama's dead."

SOUTHERN PECAN PIE

A SIBLEY-ELLIS FAMILY RECIPE

From the kitchen of Corrie Robert Lee Freeman Sibley

SOUTHERN PECAN PIE

Ingredients:

"¼ slab of butter" = ½ cup or 1 stick of butter
1 cup sugar

1 cup Karo syrup

4 eggs, beaten

1 TSP vanilla

¼ TSP salt

2 pie shells

1 cup pecan halves

Directions:

Combine butter, sugar, and Karo syrup

in a pot and cook over low heat, stirring

continuously, until sugar is dissolved.

Let cool.

Combine beaten eggs with vanilla and

salt, then add to cooled syrup mixture.

Pour mixture into pie shells and top with pecan halves.

Cook until pie crust is brown.

CRYSTAL MCGOUGH, SHARING ABOUT CORRIE ROBERT LEE FREEMAN SIBLEY

"My grandparents were apparently pecan farmers. That's something I never knew.

"Of course, when I would visit their house (which was quite often throughout my school-aged-years), there were always tons of pecan trees. And pecans falling from trees. And pecans littering the ground (watch your step!). Not to mention that inside their house was the biggest collection of nutcrackers — the real deal, not the Christmas decoration — I have ever seen in a single location.

"But as is the case for most kids, none of these things stood out as "different" or 'unusual' to me. Neither for good or bad; strange or special. It was just my grandparents' house, and that was that.

"I hold fondly the memories of walking the property with my Grandaddy, collecting nuts from the ground, him showing me how to tell the good ones from the bad ones, and to leave the ones the birds and squirrels beat us to.

"I remember vaguely him teaching me the proper way to hold a nutcracker and crack a nut.

"And I remember warmly the pecan pies my mother would pull fresh from the oven, gooey and chewy, sweet and salty, and always with a slight crunch."

APPLES OF MY PIE

A SECOND SON BRINGS HIS DARLING HOME

Life of Pies, #2

C. S. Johnson

CHAPTER TWO

Asher Davidson

We've been on the road for nearly two hours, and I haven't been able to stop smiling the entire time. That's how I know I'm truly in love.

I look over at the beautiful woman beside me, and it's a wonder I haven't wrecked yet; I could drink in the sight of Pamela Pearson all day long and still thirst for more. Even sitting in the passenger seat, she's a portrait of grace and confidence. Her strawberry blonde hair is a perfect mix between red and gold, while her eyes are green and glowing. A smattering of freckles marks her cheeks and nose. She says she hates them, but I find them endearing. Her face is a treasure map, beckoning me to pursue each dotted trail like a pirate looking for gold.

"You okay, hun?" Pamela asks, looking a bit worried as she grips the armrest.

My smile somehow widens; I almost hate to tell her bad driving is part of my charm. Having been born in Alabama and living in Atlanta, statistically I am among the most free and angry drivers in America, outside of Texas and California.

"I'm more than okay," I assure her, reaching for her hand. She gives it to me willingly, and I feel another rush of adrenaline as she relaxes, ever so slightly, at my touch. "Are you doing okay?"

"Yes. I guess I'm a little sleepy."

I quickly nod in understanding. For the first time in the months we've been together, both of us took this week off from our jobs. However, that doesn't stop us from working at home. Early this morning, I read over some contracts while Pamela took some client calls and sent emails to her professors. "Take a nap, if you want."

"Will you be okay if I do?" She bites her lip and looks down at herself, likely more worried about wrinkles than me; she's wearing a flower-patterned dress under a white blazer, and I'm more than grateful she decided not to wear heels. "I can stay up and talk if you want."

"No, go ahead and nap. We've got a few hours till we get to Fairmont, and you'll want to be refreshed and ready when you meet my family. Mama texted me a little while ago and told me Matthias is there."

"Your brother is actually home?" Pamela's eyes widen and blink in surprise, and it perfectly echoes how I'd felt in hearing the news. "Well, miracles happen, I guess."

I can't argue with her logic; after all, it was a miracle that Pamela and I had met at all.

We are both students at Georgia State, although I'm a month short of graduating with my bachelors in business, and she's working on her masters in psychology. We'd met at a networking seminar held over the winter interim. It was supposed to be a lecture on networking practices and career tips, but most of us signed up for prospective job leads.

That's why I'd shown up with a large pan of Mama's best mini-pie apple tarts. I figured I'd make myself stand out, for good or for ill, and I'd make a lasting impression.

And I did, especially when I didn't have enough tarts for everyone, given the large amount of interest the tarts garnered on a Saturday morning.

Honestly, I should've expected that; it was my mama's recipe, after all.

I quickly promised more for anyone willing to connect with me over job connections, and I'm happy to report that I made a lot of job-friends that day. Mama's cooking has always been like magic in that way.

And then Pamela came up to meet me.

It was like getting struck by lightning.

She was an elegant, practical woman, still feminine but professional, and I could see from her outfit—a prim, well-put-together pantsuit—she was the picture of a business success story in the making. All of this only made her more breathtaking to me, a non-traditional business major with a financing minor.

In that moment, everything else around her blurred over, and all the noise went muffled. I wasn't able to breathe properly as I firmly instructed myself to play it cool.

"I always thought food was the quickest way to a man's heart, not his business contacts," she said as she shook my hand. "Perhaps I should've brought something, too."

"I wouldn't worry about it." I laughed lightly, awed by how soft her palms were. "I'm a boring finance guy. I'll need help getting a job. You'll have an easier time of that than me, no apple tarts required."

"Why?" She arched her brow, and I knew I was about to be tested like never before. "Because I'm a woman?"

I held out my hand, and cooperatively, she handed me a copy of her resume. I took in the details: counselor-in-training, with a minor in business, electives in Spanish and foreign languages, working on her masters. After I skimmed through the other impressive sections, I looked back up at her. "All this is yours … Pamela?"

I said her name with the unabashed reverence she fully deserved, but her lips tightened almost unperceptively at my question.

"I wouldn't lie," she insisted.

I nearly laughed again. She was just so adorable, but I didn't dare say so; that was absolutely the last thing she wanted to hear.

"Well then, since this is yours, you'll definitely have an easier time getting a job than I will. Not because you're a woman, but because you're a smart, capable, accomplished woman."

I handed her resume back to her, and she took it back with a begrudging amount of respect.

"Well, I can't say you're wrong," she said with a small smile this time. "But time will tell if you're right about the job market."

Some amount of bold amusement and daring stirred up inside of me. "How about we bet on it?"

She eyed me carefully, clearly amused. "Aren't you a business major? I thought betting went against your creed."

"We can call it an investment," I replied, holding an apple tart out to her.

She eyed it carefully, as if knowing I meant to follow up my offering with requests for her contact information, her email, her phone, or really anything at all.

When she finally reached forward a few seconds later, I knew I'd won her over— if only for a single, first small step.

Her fingers brushed against mine lightly, and it was enough to spark a fire inside of my heart.

It wasn't long after the seminar we officially started dating.

By the end of the semester, a lifetime of three months later—three months of coffee dates, late night dinners, study sessions, research adventures, arguing over movies, books; hinting at our backstories, tentatively planning our future, while celebrating the present; Pamela getting an internship with a counseling center before I got offered a job and then arguing over whether or not I lost our initial bet—I'd never met anyone who made me felt even remotely close to how I feel when I looked at Pamela.

And today, I'm finally getting my return on my investment: Pamela agreed to come home to Alabama with me to meet my family. She is a smart lady, and she likely suspects how much it means to me—and what it means for us.

I tighten her hand in mine again as we turn off the interstate and head up another highway.

The road becomes more wavy, more hilly, and more free, and I'm grateful all over again I'd sprung for a larger sedan rental. A smaller car would've been less money, but there's more room for Pamela to curl in her seat and drift off to sleep.

It's a long drive from my apartment in the heart of Atlanta to home, and I don't blame Pamela for feeling tired. Soon, I hear her snoring lightly. She never believes me when I tell her she snores, but if I ever try to record her, I'll be essentially signing my own death warrant.

Pamela is a very organized sort of woman, and she doesn't like the idea of doing anything that's outright unladylike.

I continue to sneak peeks at her as we drive. It seems very little time at all has passed before we head into rougher country roads when she blinks awake.

"Where are we?" she murmurs, running a hand over her hair to smooth it out. She straightens in her seat and pulls on her shirt, trying to erase the newly acquired wrinkles on her skirt and jacket.

"We're on Highway 43. Are you hungry?"

"A little," she admits, pursing her lips together softly.

She's uncomfortable, but polite, and I am desperate to please her.

"There's a place we can stop at a little further up the road," I tell her. "Fresh Village. It's a farmer's market, and it's always got some good stuff."

"Will it even be open? It's not harvest time." Pamela looks confused, and then she blushes a little.

Even though it's been only a few months, I know what she's thinking. She grew up in a small town in Ohio, surrounded by farms. It's similar to my own backstory, although her nearby farms grew wheat, while mine varied between beans, pecans, and peanuts. But unlike me, even with my family's checkered past full of scandals, she isn't eager to return home. When I hint that I'd like to meet her folks, she'll say that she's planning to invite them down for Easter, or perhaps the 4th of July.

Going off to college was a chance to rebrand herself, and Pamela had clearly taken the task to heart.

I clear my throat. "I've met with the owner before, and I know she'll still have fresh fruits and vegetables. I'm thinking there might even have a nice bouquet for Mama, too."

"Oh." At this, Pamela smiles and nods. "Well, all right. And we can get one for your sister, too. Her name's Samantha, right?"

"Oh, Sama would love that." Of all the people in the world I love, Mama and Sama and Pamela are all in the top three, and it makes my heart soar to hear Pamela think of my baby sister in such a sweet, thoughtful way. "Maybe we can see if they'll have some apples, too."

"Why? They're not in season."

"Fresh Village'll have some good ones. And Sama's favorite pie is apple. If we bring some home, maybe we can get Mama to enter the Pie Festival this weekend. I know she'd win, hands-down."

"She's never won?" Pamela's eyebrows raised in surprise. "I find that hard to believe."

I shrug. "Well, she never enters, and she's never said why, either. But anyway, she probably doesn't want to compete with Orpah Abraham; I know I wouldn't want to be the one to dethrone the Daytime Diva of Northeastern Alabama."

"Orpah Abraham?" Pamela's mouth drops open in genuine surprise. "Your mom knows Orpah Abraham?"

"Yeah, sort of. Pops—my papa—used to be best friends with her brother before she was famous," I explain. "But they … had a kind of falling out, more than a decade ago. Now Orpah's brother's running her overseas charity in Africa. Mama doesn't like dealing with the bad blood between all them, especially after Sama was born. She says it makes everyone upset, and Sama most of all."

"But I thought your dad wasn't around?" Pamela frowns again.

I can really only nod out a reply, and I suddenly feel awkward; both Pamela and I have talked about our pasts, but really, only in the most general of terms. Pamela doesn't like to revisit her past that much, and I don't exactly want to tell her mine. She is a psychology major, someone who wants to help people with their problems. Pamela was a psychology major, someone who wanted to help people with their problems. And my family and I have problems, for sure, but they aren't the kind that are settled with therapy.

"I'm sorry." The awkward silence is finally over as Pamela takes my arm and pats it comfortingly. "How old were you?"

Despite her kindness, I keep my gaze firmly on the road. "I was twelve."

I hear the words leave my mouth with ease, but on the inside, I feel like a gravedigger hoisting up the last shovel of dirt.

I am not that twelve-year-old poor boy without a father anymore, but he's still part of me. He's the reason I never want to be poor again, the reason I waited so long to go off to college, and the reason, above all, I want to be a good father to my children.

"I'm sorry." Pamela leans her head on my shoulder this time. I'm grateful for her comfort, but I'm also grateful she doesn't ask about Pops anymore.

It's a sore subject.

I clear my throat, ready to change the subject. "So, yeah, let's see if we can find some apples good enough to get Mama to enter the pie contest this year, right, darling?"

"Will do. I remember her tarts." Pamela gives me a flirtatious smile, and I know she's thinking of the day we met, too. "Even if she doesn't enter the contest, maybe she can show me how to make those while we're here."

"I would love that." I start to cheer up again as I turn off the highway to head into the Fresh Village Farmer's Market.

Once we're parked, I jump out to help Pamela out of the car like a gentleman, but she waves me away.

"I don't know why you do that," she says with a laugh. "Women can get out of cars by themselves."

"I just like having the chance to make you feel special," I reply with a grin. It's an old bit between us. "Why shouldn't a man like me be willing to make any excuse to be near you?"

"More like make any excuse to touch me."

"Well, I'll plead the fifth on that," I say, taking her hand and placing a kiss on the back of her hand.

She blushes and then looks toward the shop. I can see the excitement dim in her eyes as she stands there.

It's a little more worn down and shoddy than the last time I'd stopped, but it's still the same old place I remember. The driveway is cracked where it's paved, with plenty of parking on the dirt and grass nearby. Not far off, there are some cows and an old horse eating in a field. The wooden house and its pavilion are painted with a dark red and navy design. I can see the hesitation in her eyes as she looks at it.

"This is going to be one of our adventures, isn't it?" Pamela asks as she looks around dubiously.

"We're already on an adventure," I remind her.

She mumbles out something non-committedly and I take her arm like a gentleman, just as Mama taught me.

We walk inside the pavilion and immediately, fresh fruits and vegetables and flowers all fight over whose scent is the strongest.

I soon forget about the smell as I spy all my favorite sweets. I'm examining the moon pies and cobblers as Pamela sticks beside me.

"Hey, Asher, who owns all this, anyway?" she asks, her voice no louder than a whisper. "The Dukes of Hazzard? A KKK shareholder?"

"What do you mean?" I glance over to see her eying the fireplace at the end of the room. Over the center of is a very old, framed Confederate Flag. "Oh, that? That's Memaw's."

"Memaw's?" Pamela's face looks pained as I gesture toward a nearby portrait of an elderly black woman. "She's a KKK member?"

"No, of course not. But her neighbor, Bobby Frank, had a great-great-grandpap who was. It's actually a really cool story." I lead her down a new aisle, eager to examine the various apple displays. "Memaw's family's owned this land since the Civil War ended and Reconstruction began. Bobby Frank's great-great grandpap was a Dixiecrat who was outraged when Lincoln freed the slaves."

"I can imagine," Pam says as she wrinkles her nose. She glances back at the framed Confederate Flag. "Is this his flag?"

"It's actually Memaw's great-grandpap's. He fought for the Confederacy for his freedom. Once the war ended, he became a free man. The Confederate soldiers were

all adopted by law into the United States army, so Memaw says her relatives technically served in the United States Army."

"I didn't know that," Pamela murmurs, but I barely hear her, as I try to repeat what Memaw had told me before about the history here.

"Bobby Frank's great-grand-pap found Jesus a few years after the war ended. Memaw's family had been sharecropping with some of the other freed slaves by then, and when a drought hit, he cosigned a loan so Memaw's family could survive. Ever since then, no matter the divide, no matter how hard the times, they've weathered the good and the bad together."

"That sounds almost like a fairy tale of sorts," Pamela says.

"Well, why shouldn't it, doll baby? America is a land of second chances."

I smile at the sound of old Memaw's voice, and I whirl around to see her as she huffs her way out to meet me. We've met a few times before on my trips home at the end of my semesters, and she was a sweet old lady that reminded me of sunshine and tobacco.

"Mr. Asher, what's this yank talking about? You angry about my flag?" She frowns at Pamela as she points to the flag on the wall. "My great-grand-pappy kept that flag as a piece of history. He was a proud soldier, and he knew just 'cause you start life out in one place don't mean that's where you end up."

Pamela looks utterly confused and embarrassed now, and I maneuver in front of her to give her a moment to recoup while I give my regards to Memaw.

"It's nice to see you again, Miss Memaw," I say, pretending to dip my imaginary cap to her. She giggles like a little girl as wrinkles line up along her ebony skin before breaking off into a cough. "This is Pamela, my girlfriend."

"Girlfriend? You? You must be joking, Mr. Asher." Memaw smiles, but then she eyes Pamela critically. I'm surprised when she sighs a moment later. "She's a real beaut, though. Hard to compete against that."

"Well, if I asked you out, your kids would think I'm trying to steal their inheritance."

Memaw lets out a full-bellied laugh, and I join in. Beside me, I see Pamela smile, although she's still hesitant.

Memaw pats my arm. "Well, I suppose this calls for a celebration." She examines Pamela again, running her eyes over her whole body, from the top of her head down to the demure flats on her feet. "Pick some apples on the house, since you've got a reason to celebrate."

"Thank you!" I grin excitedly, while Pamela only turns red and pulls her blazer more tightly around her. "Sama will be grateful."

"I know it." Memaw gives me a nod and a wink. She gives me a quick wave, and then limps toward the back of the pavilion. "Nice seeing you again, Mr. Asher."

"You, too, ma'am." I look back over at Pamela, surprised she's not smiling. "What is it?"

She flinches, and it's only when Memaw is out of earshot that Pamela says anything. "That lady thinks I'm pregnant, doesn't she?"

"Are you?" I ask, suddenly overjoyed at the thought.

"No, of course not."

"Oh." My happiness dips just the slightest, but I'm determined not to let it bother me. We were on our way to see Mama, so I could propose, and babies and family and a new house and a real home couldn't be too far off. But the look on Pamela's face makes me a little uncomfortable, for some reason. "Would you be upset if you were?"

"Would you be upset if I was?" Pamela gives me a teasing smile, trying to brush it off. "After all, maybe it's not yours. It's not like we're married."

"Yet." I take her hand again, and she goes completely still for a moment. I give her a teasing look, as I move in closer, like I am going to get down on one knee and ask her then and there.

"Asher," she whispers. "I had a feeling you would propose, but please … not here. Not here where there's a racist flag framed behind us and people think I'm pregnant."

"Well, how could I resist a request like that?" I chuckle. "But really, Memaw explained why she has the flag, and it's just a part of history. And as for the people, they probably have to assume you're pregnant for you to be stuck with someone like me. I'm clearly out of your league."

"That's true," Pamela agrees, relaxing just a little once more. "But I still don't like it. I don't want to be a barefoot and pregnant breeder. People shouldn't push that kind of idea onto women."

"Well, they're probably not going to push it onto men," I say, and she just frowns at me again.

"I don't want to talk about it anymore," she says in that prim, professional tone of hers. I usually think it's an admirable trait of hers, but this time, it's grating—just a little. "Let's just get out of here. This place makes me lose my appetite."

I nod, and together, we head up to pay for the small handfuls of sweets I'd gathered, two full bouquets of flowers for Mama and Sama, and under Memaw's direction, I get an entire basket of red apples at no cost. As we head out to the car, I think about how bright and cheery they look, with their shiny skin and distinctive color.

Pamela takes them from me and shoves them into the backseat, and for the first time, I see how careless she can be. It's then I start to question myself, wondering if I am feeling okay, or if I am imagining things, or if I am in denial.

I'm probably in denial, because something feels like it's mysteriously wrong.

Pamela and I leave the farmer's market in silence, and the silence continues as we drive up toward Fairmont. The road continues, and this time, as I sneak peeks at Pamela, she's sitting there, still looking pretty, but the same level of excitement is no longer there.

I don't want to do this … I don't want to ask her.

But I have to. Don't I?

I dare myself to just say it, but there's no joy in the dare as I speak. "Okay, I know you didn't want to talk about it anymore, but I thought you wanted kids."

"I do," she replies quickly. "Just like I want to be married one day, but I don't want to be proposed to in a Confederate outlet mall."

"Is that it?"

"I guess I don't want to be married to a degenerate, either," she says.

"Are you calling me a degenerate, or is that just a general observation?"

"Asher, please."

"Pamela, please." I bite back a sigh. "Look, I love you. I really do. I've been so happy these past few months. I just want to know we want the same things."

"Well, we do." She glances out the window. "We both wanted to have families in the future. I'm just not ready for it now."

She lays her hands across her stomach, and I suddenly wonder if she was telling me the truth earlier about being pregnant. When I press her on the subject, she only scoffs at me.

"Please stop. No, I'm not pregnant, and I've never been. But I don't want people thinking I am. What would your mother think of me then?" She wrinkles her nose before I can assure her Mama would be more gracious than Pamela expected.

I have to stop myself from laughing. Pamela is so worked up on giving my mother her best impression, she's making herself spiral into absurdity. It's amusing to me, watching a nearly-trained counselor breach her own barriers, but before I can assure her everything was fine, she keeps going.

"And what will happen if I do get pregnant?" she asks. "And what if we find out the baby is defective?"

Her words strike me hard, and things are no longer so amusing.

"Wait, stop." I frown. "What do you mean by 'defective?'"

"You know what I mean. Not compatible with life. Brain dead. Disfigured. Mentally disabled."

"Mentally disabled?" My hands are shaking on the wheel, and even though we are only a few miles from my home, I need a break.

"You know, like one with Down Syndrome baby, or even low-functioning autism. Those types of things. Your mother would hate me if I got an abortion."

I swerve off to the side of the road, and Pamela is already asking me what's wrong.

"Are you hurt? What's wrong?" she asks, confused. "What happened?"

"Let me get this straight," I say slowly. "You would abort our baby if it had Down's?"

She gives me an incredulous look; she's irritated by my bad driving even more, and then she's angry she has to answer my question.

Finally, she shrugs and holds out her hands, palms up. "Look, Asher, I know some people are upset about these kinds of situations, but they happen. I don't want kids right now. Even if we were married, we couldn't afford it, let alone having one with disabilities. I just don't see it as a good idea."

"But you would abort the baby?" I ask again, slowly trying to wrap my head around her words.

"Come on, don't be like that. It's a woman's right to choose these things. What if I was raped? Are you going to raise a baby that's not yours?"

Pamela keeps talking, trying to say all these things about how hard it is to raise kids, how women shouldn't be pushed into motherhood against their will, and how I should be more sensitive.

She doesn't seem to realize that I've gone silent.

She's still talking as I shrink into myself and slowly put the car back into drive and continue toward Fairmont.

I barely acknowledge the giant, gaudy sign showing Orpah Abraham's face; I hardly take notice of an unknown car in the driveway as I pull into Mama's.

All I can think of is how I'm no longer sure of asking Pamela to marry me.

"Asher, what's wrong with you?" Pamela asks. Her voice is much fiercer as I stop the car. "I'm sorry this last little leg of the trip was unpleasant, but aren't you going to talk to me at all before we meet with your family?"

"I don't know." That's all I can say, and that's the honest to God truth. I get out of the car, and this time I don't open Pamela's door for her.

I'm stunned, and I'm in a daze as I head for Mama's front door.

Once I get to the door, I stop; it hits me, hard, that I should probably say something after all.

Behind me, I hear Pamela get out of the car, and perhaps as an act of contrition, she gets the bucket of apples out of the backseat. I glance over to see her collect a few from off the floor.

For a split second, I think maybe I can reason with her; I think maybe if I tell her about Sama and Mama, she'd be more understanding to babies born from rape and Down Syndrome, and why I'd been so upset with her.

But before I can say anything, Sama comes barreling out the front door.

"Asher!" Her wide-set eyes, the same sparkling brown I'd remembered all my life, are full of tears.

"Don't cry, Sama," I whisper into her brown curls as I clutch her tightly. I've almost forgotten how short she is compared to me, but she fits easily under my arms. In truth, she's family, and it's too easy for me to forget her physical features as I remember how in our younger days, she used to cuddle with me for hours when I was sick, how angry she'd been with me for moving away for college, and how I promised her I would always be there for her if she needed me.

She had always been my baby sister—no matter who her real father was—and I'd always tried to do my best by her. "I'm here. I'm home."

"Your phone must be dead." Sama's slurrish words are muffled and broken as she clings to my shirt. "I have been calling you for hours."

"I'm sorry." Sama steps back from me and I feel more than guilty, knowing I'd put the phone on silent to surprise Mama—and so I wouldn't be torn away from Pamela.

Behind me, Pamela lets out a small squeak.

I look back at Pamela, only to see her gaping at Sama, studying my baby sister's brownish skin, brown curls, flattened nose, high hairline, and slanted eyes.

I don't have to ask why she's just standing there, her mouth open, and her eyes full of tears. She looks at me, and for a split second, our eyes meet.

There are tears in her eyes as she looks away and her lips press more firmly together.

The bright, beautiful picture I'd imagined for us only a few hours ago evaporates, and I'm no longer sure of what to say or what to do. Pamela and I were supposed to spend all week here with my family, going to the Pie Festival, meeting my old community members, and planning our future together.

What am I supposed to do now?

"Asher." Sama grips my arms, as if she knows.

I expect her to ask about Pamela, and I'm prepared to tell her about the flowers we got at Fresh Village and the apples, too.

But what she tells me is the very last thing I expected to hear.

"Mama's dead, Asher." Sama's eyes spill over with tears. "Mama's dead."

I grip her back as she cries, once more trying to get my mind to accept her words. "What?"

The door to the house opens up, and there's Matthias—my older brother who's aged considerably since the last time I saw him—standing at the door.

"Samantha's right. Mama died. I don't know what happened."

That's when I notice he's been crying, too.

My hardened, cynical, spiteful brother has been crying.

It's then my world truly begins to fall apart.

"Did you call the police?" I ask, trying to remember there are procedures to follow, that there are things to be done.

"It happened a little while ago," Matthias says, his words tense and mumbling. "But I checked. She's dead."

"I … I can't believe … " I shake my head, trying to clear my thoughts. "What happened?"

"I called Pip." Sama frowns at Matthias. "He's not happy about that, but Pip is coming to help."

Slowly, I nod, but my mind is losing its grip on reality. "Judge Piper is coming here," I say, trying to force myself to think things through.

It's then I hear the police sirens and a pristine, white-pearl Cadillac pulls up to the front of the house. An older man, with a pudgy belly, dark skin, and gray-white hair nearly falls out of the driver's seat. He looks from me to Matthias to Sama to Pamela, all confused.

"Where's Martha?" he asks, and I barely have time to recognize Judge Piper as Sama leaves my arms and heads into his.

He grips her tightly in a hug as she babbles to him about what happened. Meanwhile, Matthias looks angry, Pamela looks shocked, and I am just standing there, unable to do anything but stare at the bucket full of apples in Pamela's arms.

They'd seemed so happy and fresh earlier, but now, their colors only seem faded and dry. Their shine disappears along with my daydreams, and the nightmares begin.

There's one last line of light. Judge Piper puts his hand on my shoulder.

"I'll help you with this," he tells me. He starts asking some questions, but his assurance is all I hear before I fall to my knees and let out a heart-breaking sob.

MAMA MAGOO'S FRESH APPLE PIE

A MCGOUGH FAMILY RECIPE

From the kitchen of Crystal McGough

MAMA MAGOO'S FRESH APPLE PIE

Ingredients:

1 9-inch pie pan

2 9-inch pie shells

¾ cup sugar

¼ cup flour

½ TSP nutmeg

½ TSP cinnamon

Dash of salt

6 cups thinly sliced pared tart apples

(approximately 5 medium apples)

2 TBSP butter or margarine

Pre-heat oven to 425° F. Line pie pan with one uncooked pie crust pastry.

Mix sugar, flour, nutmeg, cinnamon, and salt.

Lightly toss apples in sugar and seasoning mixture until apples are fully-coated.

Put apple mixture into pastry-lined pie pan and dot with butter.

Place second pie crust pastry on top and pinch/flute the edges to seal the two crusts together.

Using a knife, carve small slits into the top pie crust.

Cover edges of pie with 2-3-inch strips of aluminum foil to prevent excessive browning.

Remove foil during the last 15 minutes of baking.

Bake 40-50 minutes or until crust is brown and juices begin to bubble through the slits in the crust.

Optional: Serve warm, with vanilla-bean ice cream.

from
<u>CRYSTAL MCGOUGH</u>

"When my husband and I were newlyweds, we were poor. Dirt poor. Ramen-eating-college-kids poor. So, like any poor, newly married college kids, we never said no to free food. Even if "free food" meant enough apples to fill up two mini-fridges and one full-sized refrigerator/freezer combo, with stacks of apple-filled boxes left over. I don't remember who gave us all the apples (some kind soul from our church, I'm sure), but apparently apples were to be our life-bread for the foreseeable future.

"I'm not much of a cook, personally, but I decided we needed to make use of as many apples as possible before they went to waste. So, to the kitchen I went. I experimented with multiple recipes, many failing, before finally being able to serve up something that was more than just edible — it was delicious. Now, I'll admit, my first success was far from beautiful. It ended up looking like a pile of cinnamon-apple-pastry slop, with ice cream on the side. But, oh boy, how my new husband and I loved it! He was so impressed, he invited his mom over so I could make another for her. That one came out a little better looking than its predecessor and still tasted every bit as good.

"After many more pies and cobblers, side dishes and entrees, and occasionally just grabbing an apple here and there for a quick snack, one-by-one the (probably several hundred) apples began to dwindle. It was quite an experience, living off apples and Ramen for a year or two, but we'll always be grateful to those who fed us in any capacity until we got on our feet. And of course, any chance we get, we're happy to pay it forward."

PIED PIPER

A GUARDIAN OF JUSTICE FACES A NEW TRIAL

Life of Pies, #3

C. S. Johnson

CHAPTER THREE

Judge Charles "Pip" Piper

The day started out so slowly.

Ever since my lovely wife, Michelle, passed on eight years ago, I'd woken up just as I always had. The air was crisp with the early morning chill, the house was empty, and my bones were aching. Over the years my eyes had grown weaker, my middle had gotten larger, my fingers moved more stiffly, and my youth had chipped away.

But that's life, and since I'm alive, there's work to be done and things to do.

And so I set out to do them, even if I move a bit slower in getting them done.

Things are the way they are, and they don't change simply because we wish them to. A man needs to work, and so I have mine.

This morning at Fairmont City Hall, I delivered my latest controversial verdict, which meant deciding to try a minor as an adult after he'd sold drugs and poison, before murdering his neighbor with a mix of hemlock and ricin.

After dismissing the court, I filed my paperwork, packed up my briefcase, and left the building.

It's not joy I feel as I leave, but relief.

I walk into the bank next door. I see Garland Morris is here, and quickly enough, he begins pushing for double-or-nothing on our latest bet.

"Come on, Charles," he practically pleads, as I spot the opportunistic gleam in his eye. "My luck is bound to change."

"Yes," I agree. "It'll get worse."

"Not this time, I swear."

"That's poor reasoning to use with a judge who's been on the bench as long as I have, and you know it."

"You're a real stick in the mud." Morris pretends to scowl at me before he grins. "What's one more bet?"

He'd said that the last time, too. That's how our original fifty-dollar bet back in February morphed into a pot of a thousand dollars two months later.

I arch my brow. "You know, it's fortunate that I'm around to keep you straight, or I'd be worried about a banker with a gambling problem."

Morris laughs. "Maybe I'm just using you as a cover, huh?"

"Maybe." I smile back as I pull out my latest paycheck and hand it to him to deposit.

Thirty-two years hasn't changed my routine much, even if age has made me slower and technology has made life easier.

Each payday I give Morris my paycheck, request a few bills for the week, and make chit-chat for a time. Morris will inevitably mention his latest interest and try to make a game out of it with me, which is how our betting tradition began.

Even if I'm the winner more often than not, I admire Morris' enthusiasm. He always seeks out new things to learn or do or enjoy, while I tend to stick to what I know. Our friendship isn't something I'd expect, so I appreciate him, and I get the feeling others like how we get along, too. The two of us are pillars among the other folks here in town, and not just because of our jobs.

Morris and I grew up in Fairmont, seeing the disgraces of racism and how the Civil Rights movement, along with individual mercy, slowly brought the once-segregated town together. Had things gone differently, a white man like Morris and a black man like me wouldn't have been friends at all.

"Come, now, Charles. One last round for this month? The Fairmont Spring Festival starts today, and it'll be a good way to celebrate."

"I guess I shouldn't stop a man who's eager to give me his money." I eye him carefully, sizing him up. "If you're eager to go double-or-nothing, I'll bet you have an inside tip."

"Sure do." Morris leans in a little closer. "I hear your Martha's finally entering the pie contest this year, and I'm betting she'll be the winner at last."

"My Martha?" My heart finally stirs to life, genuinely surprised and pleased to arrive at its favorite topic, but I only scowl at Morris.

"Yes, *your* Martha." Morris chuckles. "You mean she didn't tell you? And here I thought you were supposed to be sweet on each other. Did you two have a fight?"

"A man's business is his own," I grumble, more out of habit than anything else.

It's been over a decade since her husband up and left, and the rumors about us began.

The rumors are especially scornful and wicked, since some of them are true. Just like Morris, Martha and I grew up in Fairmont. Back in our younger days, we'd always been cordial, even if society said we weren't supposed to go together. Eventually, our lives took us on separate paths: Martha married her husband, and I married my wife. But when her divorce was final, I came back into her life, and she came back into mine.

At first, it was all business: I represented Martha in court, so she could get child support from her ex. But then, gradually, we became real friends, and things became more personal.

"You know that's what the rumors always say," I add, frowning. I'd said the same thing to my wife, too, and on more than one occasion; Michelle hadn't liked Martha at all, and that only ended up fueling the gossip more. "Martha won't really enter the contest. She wouldn't risk stepping on Orpah Abraham's toes."

Morris nudges my arm. "You gonna ask her when you see her tonight?"

I glare at him in warning, and then calmly tuck my money into my coat pocket, pick up my briefcase, and nod more graciously than I'd like. "See you later, Morris. And speaking of our friendly bets, let's get lunch soon. You can pay, to help offset your losses."

I'm halfway to the exit when Morris calls out to me again. "Scared Martha will lose to the Pie Queen, Charles? Or don't you want to bet against her?"

I stop and grip the handle on my suitcase. Most people in town never dare to push when it comes to me and Martha.

"Clarice Youngblood herself told me it's true," he adds, likely knowing it would bother me.

For a long moment, I'm still and silent.

And then I turn around.

"Alright, Morris. Double or nothing," I say. "But no cancelling your bet once you find out Martha's not entering the contest."

If I know anything in this world now, it's Martha. And she will not enter the contest.

She wouldn't do that.

Morris is too happy to say much else, and I do not want to even consider the possibility I am wrong.

My Cadillac gleams brightly in the springtime sun, and the sight of it makes me smile.

My family never had it easy. We'd always worked as hard for our money as much as our dignity, even if neither were within reach. My Pa was a plumber, just as my great-grandpa had been a plumber, and we knew what it was to clean up the worst parts of society and human nature. I was the first in my family to opt for a different path; I was the first son in my family to go to college. I'd offered Pa the Cadillac, and he'd driven it around until he'd died a few years back.

Martha had brought me a chocolate pie for his wake, and she'd waited until everyone else was gone before she'd sit and talk with me as I ate it.

"This is great," I remember saying, just as much as I remember the smooth, crumbly taste of her pie.

"The bitterness of the chocolate pairs well with its sweetness," Martha explained. "That's one of the mysteries of life, the nature of its paradoxes." She smiled brightly. "And that's one of the secrets to great baking, too."

"This is better than Orpah Abraham's pies," I told her, taking another bite. "And I would know. I've been a judge on the pie panel for the last six years."

"Well, we both know I wouldn't want to upset Orpah," Martha told me gently. "And it's enough for me that you like it. I made it for you."

She put her hand on mine and squeezed it. "You've always been there for me when I needed you and your judging talents. So I'm glad I can at least pay you back, as small as it is."

"This is no small thing," I assured her, taking another bite of her pie.

We said little else that night, but I've never forgotten that moment.

I'd been desperately sad at my Pa's passing; it'd reminded me too much of losing Michelle. But I also remember heading home, with half a pie left in the pie pan, feeling more hopeful than I had in years.

I open the car door and sit down in the driver's seat, already whistling a happy tune.

As much as I hate others commenting on my relationship with Martha, including Morris, he is right.

I *am* going to see her tonight.

And I *am* excited to see her.

My heart soars in anticipation, and not just for the whisky and homemade pie I am certain she has waiting for me.

Tonight is the night she's finally going to tell her children about us.

Once I get to her house, I will ask about the rumors of her entering the pie contest.

She wouldn't do that … would she?

I know she's finally ready to put the past behind her, and she's open to a future, too.

But even still, entering that contest doesn't seem like a good idea at all.

As I get into my car, my cell phone rings. I groan and scramble to get it out of my back pocket, muttering a string of incoherent curses until I accept the call.

It's Martha's home number, and my face crinkles with a wide smile as I say hello.

"Pip?"

My smile falters just a little, before it comes back just as strong. "Sama?"

"Pip!"

Even in light of the circumstances, my heart skips with added love and affection in hearing Sama call for me. She's the only one who's ever called me "Pip," and I love her all the more for it.

"Sama-Girl."

"Pip, get over here quick. Something's wrong with Mama."

I frown. "What is it?"

Her voice is a little stuttered, but still strong. "I think … Mama's dead."

"What?"

Sama explains that Martha fell over and didn't wake up, and then something about Matthias and Asher. I'm not sure what she's saying, but then her voice breaks and she starts sobbing.

All I can hear is her saying that Martha is dead.

No.

Today is supposed to be the first day in over a decade I would be coming home to a woman who loved me. I hope Sama is wrong, but she's always been a bright, happy, smart, little girl. And there isn't any reason she would lie to me.

No.

"I'm coming," I say. "Call an ambulance, and anyone else you can. I'll be there soon."

I hang up and put the car in drive.

I know the way to Martha's house, and I drive there without thought or feeling. The streets blur over as I pass by the Street Market, the Fairmont Veterans

Association, the Presbyterian church, the African church, and then the Vietnamese Catholic church.

I turn at Fairmont City Park, and that's when I speed up. Her house is close, and behind me I can hear a police siren and an ambulance.

Dread starts slipping in past my hardened defenses.

I pull up to Martha's house; there are two cars in the driveway I don't recognize.

"Judge Piper? Is that you?"

A new voice calls to me, and I see Edith Hennessey walk out onto her front porch. She's curious, but I don't have time to talk.

"Edith, can you come help?" I ask. "Sama says something's wrong."

"What is it?"

"I don't know for sure, just come!" I snap, before racing for the door, ignoring her frightened flinching.

Edith's husband has given her enough reason to hate men yelling at her over the years.

I'll apologize later.

"Sama?" I open the door and brace myself. "Where's Martha?"

It doesn't take more than a second to see everything.

The scene before me is even more horrible than I could've imagined.

Martha's body lay across the small kitchen floor. She's still and unmoving; her hair, a gray-streaked blonde, is splayed in a mess of tangles.

There's a mess of food on the floor alongside her.

I glance at the kitchen counters, oddly aware of her quaint little figurines and industry grade food prep machines; they almost make me smile, as I think of how the Martha I know is a woman of complicated pleasures.

My gaze goes from the food scraps around the sink to the piles of plates to the half-packed bags of leftovers. She'd spent all day cooking her best recipes. She knew we were going to have a hard day ahead of us, likely with mixed results as Matthias came home and Asher brought his lady friend to meet everyone.

I put my hand on my forehead, pressing hard against my eyes.

Martha wanted to be prepared to tell everyone that we're dating.

"Pip!"

"Sama … what happened?" I ask, as she practically leaps into my arms.

"Mama was just cleaning up and she fell over," Sama says. Her puffy cheeks are wet with tears and her brown eyes are red, and I can tell she's been trying hard not to pull at her tight, dark curls.

The rumors have swirled for years that she's biologically mine, and while I've said nothing to answer them, I do love her as my own.

"Judge Piper."

I see another man—Matthias, Martha's oldest son, as he stares over at me coldly.

It's been over ten years since he was caught with drugs and I sentenced him to community service, but he clearly didn't appreciate my light sentencing from the look of it. There's a hard line across his sunburned-brow, but I can see the softness in his blue eyes as he looks down at Martha on the floor. I recall Martha's latest concerns about getting calls from some loan sharks.

"Matthias," I murmur, trying to be as polite as I can manage—for Sama's sake, if nothing else, although she seems to be the one who needs it the least. Over on the other side of the kitchen, I recognize Asher, Martha's second son, who looks weak at the knees. In the other corner, there's a redheaded woman who seems to know how out of place she is.

I'm guessing that this is Asher's girlfriend or fiancée, and she's apparently as shell-shocked as the rest of them.

Shell-shocked, useless. Same thing in this case.

Gently, I press a kiss to the top of Sama's head. "Let me help Asher," I whisper, and she nods in understanding.

As I put my hand on Asher's shoulder, I notice she goes and sits down on a small couch in the adjacent living room. She's crying some, but I can't help her.

Is Edith coming or not? I wonder bitterly. *She probably had to ask Donnie for permission to leave the house.*

"Asher, I'll help you with this," I say, doing my best to support the other child as I do my best to keep my cool.

The policeman and an EMT knock on the front door as Asher breaks down, falling to his knees and starting to cry.

I look over at the redheaded woman. "Patrice?" I ask, trying to recall Martha's mention of her.

"Pamela," she murmurs.

"Yes, that's right. Pamela. See if you can help him." I point down to Asher, and I'm surprised to see her wince.

I grit my teeth at her hesitation; Asher has always been a good boy. I can understand the awkwardness of our situation, but she sure seems like she doesn't know anything. The boy clearly has a weakness for her pretty face.

"If you're not able to do that," I tell Pamela in a sharp tone, "go let the cops in."

She nods quickly and heads to the door as I turn to Matthias.

Sama is distraught, and Asher is in despair. As much as he doesn't like it, Matthias and I only have each other.

"Tell me what happened," I say.

"Don't I need a lawyer, first?" Matthias snarls.

"Only if you're guilty," I snap back, and it's more clear than ever we're not going to get along.

Not that we ever did …

"I'll wait for the cops," Matthias says. "Or are they in your pocket?"

I scowl at him, but Fairmont's sheriff, Solomon McCain, is quick to offer a response.

"We're in the business of stopping crime, not making more of it," Solomon says. "And Judge Piper here doesn't need to make any more work for himself. He's getting up there in years, as you can see."

Solomon gives me a smirk, and if we'd been talking after a court case, I might've smiled back.

The EMT, a nice young man named Brady, begins checking over Martha's body, as Solomon asks the usual questions. I try to protect Sama as much as possible, and it's only when I need to that I turn to look over at Matthias expectantly.

"She'd been expecting you?" Solomon asks Matthias, who nods.

"Yes, sir."

There's a tightness to his voice that makes me feel like he's hiding something.

I narrow my eyes. Martha had mentioned to me before about his money troubles, and how with his criminal history, she was worried he'd gone down another broken road.

"When was the last time you saw her before today?" Solomon continues.

Matthias looks uncomfortable. "It's been a few years."

"Twelve, to be exact," I retort. "She's been waiting for you to come home since you left."

"Twelve years?" Solomon asks. "Why did you come home, today of all days?"

"I was just planning on it," Matthias says. His eyes are going wild. "Look, I was here earlier and she was making me lunch, and we had a nice meal and talked. That's all."

"Mama gave you the money you wanted."

Solomon, Matthias, Asher, and I all whirled around to look at Sama as she spoke.

"I saw you," she says. "She gave you a check."

Matthias' face blotched over in purple. "Well, yes, but it's not my fault she had a heart attack or something—"

"Let me see this check," I say, but Matthias balks.

"Hell, no," he snaps. "You might be *her* father, but you're sure as hell not mine."

"And you're poorer for it," I argue. "My child wouldn't be dealing drugs in Nashville while chasing some pie-in-the-sky dream of his."

"I'm a PR executive for some of the biggest up-and-coming names in the music industry," Matthias shouts back. "I'm not poor."

"I know about your debts. Martha told me."

"Gentlemen, please calm down," Solomon interrupts us sharply. "This is not the time or the place. Martha deserves better."

I shut my mouth in reply and remorse, knowing he is right.

"You can discuss paternal rights later, Charles," Solomon says.

My cheeks suddenly heat up to high temperatures. The rumors always bothered Martha, even if we were together now; she wouldn't like giving people more gossip along the grapevine. Sama already got enough grief from others due to her disabilities and her Down's Syndrome. She didn't need to worry about where I fit into her life, or where she fit into ours.

I clear my throat. "I'm not—"

"And as for you, son." Solomon cuts me off as he turns to Matthias. "How much did your mom give you?"

"That's none of your business." Matthias turned away. "That's between me and her, and no one else."

Brady spoke up. "It looks like she died of a heart attack," he says. "Sudden, and quick."

"Are you sure?" I ask.

Brady nods. "It seems to fit."

"I heard Mama had some heart problems," Matthias whispers, before he looks down at the floor again. "I didn't know how bad it was."

"She didn't have bad heart problems," Asher says. "She was taking some heart medication for high blood pressure. It's not the same thing. She shouldn't be like this."

As the two of them bicker in muted tones, I look at Martha's body. I watch as Brady puts his stethoscope on her chest, and nothing moves.

Asher winces, Matthias looks away, and Sama's thankfully in another room.

I just watch.

For years I'd seen everything from hardened criminals and young boys and girls grow old from pain, shock, despair, desperation, and disaster. As much as I love Martha, she's already becoming another dead body in my line of vision.

But when Brady pushes down on her chest, I can almost see the puff of air as it leaves her. A second later, I can smell its acrid sweetness.

A small, faint memory pops into my head from earlier. The young man's trial, who I'd demanded to be tried as an adult …

Hemlock and ricin.

Is it possible? I wonder. Is it possible she was poisoned, too?

"I want an autopsy."

I say the words as I think them, but the moment I hear them, I know it's true, and it's for the best. "Asher. Tell them you want an autopsy. Tell them to get a toxicological report for you."

"What?" Asher blinks up at me.

"I have a hunch," I tell him softly. "Get the report. You have nothing to lose."

Matthias grumbled inaudibly. "Come on, Judge Piper, that's enough. Can't you let my mother rest in peace? Haven't you given her enough grief over the years?"

"Martha was all the joy I've had in recent months," I shout, suddenly unable to keep it back any longer.

"You're just saying that because you want your money back, don't you?" Matthias lashes out at me. "I want you out of here. I'm her oldest and next of kin, so that makes this entire house mine."

"No, it doesn't," I say. "I happen to know she's written up her will for all three of you to split equally."

"Oh, really? How do you know that?" Matthias practically spits out the words.

I hold my ground, unimpressed by his outburst. "I've worked with her on multiple occasions, remember? Not just the cases against you, but also your father—"

"How dare you. How could you do this to her?" Matthias' voice is a small hiss. "First you rape her, impregnate her, buy her silence, watch as Papa runs off, and now you're trying to say you're in a relationship with her?"

"That's not true—not all true, anyway," I insist, but everyone is dead silent now. I feel them watching me, and, for once, I'm flustered; I hate that Matthias is casting me in the role of the villain, when I'd only ever been Martha's champion. "That's not what happened, and you know it."

Sama looks over at me with her large, wide-set puppy eyes. "Pip?"

"In a moment, Sama-Girl," I tell her gently, before turning back to Matthias. "That's not the truth."

"Well, I don't know who else I can believe," Matthias snaps. "Mama's dead."

"You can ask your father about Sama," I whisper softly. "But I helped her draw up her will years ago. She didn't want your father trying to take anything away from Sama. I know she left everything to all of you, equally."

Asher finally seemed to get some color back in his face. "So we need an autopsy," he says. "Sama, are you in agreement?"

We all look at her.

She doesn't handle attention like this well, and I'm not surprised when she just puts her head in her hands, pulls her knees up around her face, and ducks down.

I turn back to Matthias. "Look, Matthias, I know this is not what—"

"Hello?"

Edith finally appears in the house, just in time to interrupt me.

We all turn to look at her, and on some level, I think we're grateful for the distraction. Solomon is taking notes, and Brady is putting Martha in a black body bag.

"What in the world is going on?" Edith whispers, before she sees Martha's body on the gurney. She goes pale and looks sickly. "Oh, my. What happened?"

"We don't know, exactly," I start to say, before Matthias interrupts.

"Likely a heart attack," he says. "I know she had heart problems and some medicine issues, so it's not unexpected."

"Who told you that?" Edith asks, squinting at him. "You haven't been home in years, and I'd've known if she'd ever mentioned it."

Matthias goes oddly silent and, for once, he doesn't seem to have a quick comeback.

I look at him, now, too.

It's Pamela who finally speaks up.

"Asher, perhaps you should tell Matthias it's in his best interest to agree to an autopsy," she says quietly.

Matthias snarls at her. "I don't know who you think you are, but you're not part of this family. I want my mama to be put to rest. She's no longer in any pain, and there's no reason to believe there's foul play involved."

"Other than you showing up and needing money from her," Edith points out.

"He got it, too," I say, suddenly much more interested in what Edith had to say than I probably should've been. "Sama said he got a check from Martha."

"It's just your hush money," Matthias spat back at me. "And that doesn't have anything to do with this."

Solomon blew his whistle, forcing all of us to stop yelling at each other. "Look, I'm sure everyone is very upset," he says in the same calm, level voice I use to quiet a courtroom. "But there is reason to suspect something else happened."

All of us look at him.

"There is?" Matthias asks, his voice nearly cracking.

"Yes." Solomon points to the gravy boat. "There's some residue here that looks suspicious."

Matthias blanches over.

"I'm not saying it's proof yet," Solomon continues. "But it's worth checking out."

I take another look. After a moment of inspection, I nod bitterly. "I've seen this kind of thing before."

"Well, that's very convenient for you," Matthias scoffs.

Edith slips through the crowded kitchen as Sama starts to cry again, this time much more loudly. I watch her pull out a handkerchief and start to dab Sama's eyes kindly. I remember Martha telling me Edith had always wanted children, but she'd never been able to have kids. It's the kind of thing that only real friends know about each other. I recall Morris' comment earlier about Clarice, Martha's other best friend, and I briefly wonder if Martha had really intended to join the Pie Festival contest or not.

I look down at the pie remains littering the kitchen floor.

Pecan pie.

I look at the clock. It's getting close to evening time, and in the distance, I can almost hear the fireworks and the music of the Fairmont Pie Festival starting up as the opening ceremonies finish.

Martha will never be able to win the contest now.

Even if she'd wanted to dethrone Orpah, it's too late now. And Morris is definitely going to owe me the money now.

But his loss—and his bad luck—is nothing compared to mine.

I've lost my Martha—all of her. Her smile, her laugh, her sweetness … her pies.

Martha's pies have always been a symbol of her love, and now, I'll never get another one, or see another one, ever again.

My eyes water. A throbbing pain begins to pound inside my head and my nose prickles with pressure.

It's the same grief I'd felt at losing Pa and Michelle that washes over me now, and I am too tired to say anything, too weak to do anything, and too lonely to feel anything.

"Asher."

Thankfully, Pamela distracts us as she awkwardly stepped forward. She stands up beside Asher at last, although she doesn't touch him. Instead, she clasps her hands together in front of herself. "I think it would be best if you told Matthias—"

"I'm right here; you can just talk to me, you know," Matthias says.

Pamela straightens and clears her throat. She seems so young, but somewhat practiced at handling difficult people, and as bad as she is at it now, I want to believe there's hope for her in the future.

"I don't know much about your relationship with your mother, Matthias," she says, "but it might help everyone to get some answers with an autopsy. Even if it's not the answers they're looking for."

He's silent for a moment, and all of us are, too, besides Sama, who's still crying.

"Can't you shut her up?" Matthias grumbles.

"You know," I say, "I've dealt with criminals for over three decades now, Matthias. If you don't want an autopsy, it sure seems suspicious. And you already have a record."

Matthias looks angrier than I've ever seen him. "You saying I killed her?"

"No." I raise my brow at him. "But it is interesting you just got a lot of money from her that isn't necessarily yours anymore. Sama and Asher could contest you for it."

Asher swallowed. "I don't want any trouble. I'm happy to give it to him."

"If he agrees to an autopsy, you mean," I smoothly interrupt.

"You son of a—" Matthias' fists ball up.

"Yes," Asher agrees. "Come on, Matt. We're brothers. And we're all here together. We can handle this together."

Matthias looks helpless, and it's just a matter of waiting now.

Three minutes pass, and then he nods. "Fine. But if you think I did this just because I needed money, you're wrong. And I want a lawyer, too."

"We can get one for you," I assure him.

"You should get one for yourself," Matthias retorts. "How do we know you didn't kill her?"

Sama starts wailing, and Edith looks over at me, clearly overwhelmed.

I glare at Matthias. "Hush your mouth, boy. It's innocent until proven guilty, and let me just say it's better if you don't accidentally convict yourself—again."

Matthias' face burns beet red, but at least he finally sinks into silence.

Solomon makes some calls, Asher and Pamela exchange awkward glances, and I head over to help Edith calm Sama.

When Brady tells me they'll have the toxicology report by the end of the day tomorrow as a special favor for me, personally, I nod politely, and then tell Sama to get ready for bed.

She's exhausted and needs to go to bed.

I wish I could, too.

But my job isn't done. There's still more to do.

I help the others clean up and organize the house as best as we can; we leave the kitchen alone, since the police are still taking pictures. Some of them ask others questions, but no one has any answers that offer me any comfort.

Soon, I sit down in a chair in the living room. The place looks foreign to me, like an alien world.

Without Martha's care and love, it just seems … lifeless.

Edith tells me she'll take care of Sama for tonight, and I barely notice as Matthias sits on the couch across from me. He's angry, but he's tired, too. Asher takes Pamela upstairs to his old room, and then he comes and sits in the other chair as the hours pass. Eventually, both boys fall asleep where they're at, and I can hear Edith's quiet snoring from Sama's room.

I sit there, still awake.

My day had started slowly, but sitting here, I suddenly know this night will never truly leave me. By the time everything is quiet and dark, the only comfort I can take is knowing there's nothing else to be done—not for now, at least.

Tomorrow will bring more trouble, though.

I can already picture the news, the media, all the press and the townsfolk who will want answers—answers about Martha's death, Matthias' trouble, Asher's plans, and my role in all of it.

They'll want answers about Sama's father, too.

The thought whispers through me like a deadly chill. If there's a thought that keeps me up late into the night, it's that one.

What will they do when they find out? Will they believe me at all?

I shake my head slowly.

They'd never believed me before; I doubt they will do so now.

"Orpah's going to have a field day," I murmur, thinking of how excited she'll be to get another chance to smear me and sink my career. I can only hope she's too busy with the pie contest to worry too much about me and my role in Martha's life.

Soon, the small clock at the far end of the room echoes wearily through the room. It's three o'clock in the morning.

I take out my phone, dial my office secretary, and leave a message on her answering machine, telling her I'll be out for the next few days due to a personal matter.

She'll understand when she hears what happened to Martha.

And then I put the phone down, lean back in my chair.

Each decision I'd made over the course of my life was my own, and I gladly owned them. But now I'm guilty, convicted, and sentenced, and I hope more than anything Martha is in a better place, because I'm sure as hell not.

We'd planned to be together, after all the years we'd been apart for various reasons.

But now, our plans meant nothing. Or did they? I can't say for sure.

After all, she's gone, and I'm still here.

I put my hands over my face; my breathing comes in harsh breaths, and I finally have to step outside the house.

I'm on the porch, looking up at the dark, lonely night when a single tear finally drops down my cheek.

It's as salty and bitter as ever.

DEDE'S CHOCOLATE PIE

A ROYSTER-MCGOUGH FAMILY RECIPE

From the kitchen of Deborah Royster McGough

DEDE'S CHOCOLATE PIE

Ingredients:

1 cup sugar

3 TBSP flour (plain, white)

4 TBSP cocoa powder

3 egg yolks

½ stick of real butter

1 TSP vanilla

1 ½ cups of milk

1 pinch of salt

Bake 2 regular pie shells or 1 deep-dish pie shell and let cool.

Mix sugar, flour, and cocoa.

Add egg yolks, butter, vanilla, milk, and salt to mixture.

Cook in a thick, iron pot. (*Hopefully you have one like mine!*)

Cook on medium-high while stirring constantly.

Keep cooking at a good boil for 2 minutes, stirring the whole time.

Pour into the pie shells and cool.

Optional: Top with fresh whipped cream.

from
DEBORAH ROYSTER-MCGOUGH

"I was a teacher for 43 years, and when my sons were around the ages of 4 and 11, our neighbor's son would ride with us to school every day. As a sort-of 'thank you,' his mom gifted me with a homemade chocolate pie.

"Our whole family loved the pie so much that she gave me the recipe. To this day, I still have the same card she wrote the recipe on. I have made this chocolate pie every single Thanksgiving and Christmas since then. It's a favorite!

"My boys are now 35 and 42. I have four wonderful grandchildren from my younger son, and now they also look forward to DeDe's Chocolate Pie every Thanksgiving and Christmas."

PIE IN THE SKY

A BEREAVED NEIGHBOR TAKES A RISK

Life of Pies, #4

C. S. Johnson

CHAPTER FOUR

Edith Hennessey

The morning after death is a strange one.

Strange as it is, though, it's not strange enough to stop me from wanting a cigarette first thing.

I grit my teeth together, groaning silently as I slowly peel myself off the small rocking chair I'd used for a bed the previous night. Once I'm able to stand properly, I glance over at the sleeping teenager who'd just lost her mother. As I watch her slumbering, I thank God in his mercy for each steady breath in and breath out.

As much trouble as it'd been, I don't regret my decision to watch and stay with her. Off and on throughout the night several times, she'd woken up, sobbed and wept, and I'd comforted her as much as I could, even when it meant foregoing my own.

But no good deed goes unpunished, my back aches and my joints crackle painfully as I awkwardly tiptoe over toward the door and grab my purse off the floor, eager to get my cigarettes.

My Donnie likes to remind me of my different failings at times like these, and as I struggle with the urge to smoke, I can't say I blame him, even if it makes me feel worse.

I look back at my charge carefully once I reach the door. Samantha Davidson is a sweet girl, and nevermore so when she's sleeping. Her black, curly hair is long enough that it's spread over her pillow, and she's sucking on her fingers almost thoughtfully as she sleeps. Even when she's awake, she looks like an angel, but as I

watch her now, my heart softens, as the old longing for my own children hits me hard.

As I trip over a small worn patch in the old carpet, I have to bite my tongue to keep from cussing. Still, I hold my breath, waiting for her eyes to open.

But she doesn't.

Bless her heart.

Sama lost her mother in one moment, and then in the next, she reunited with her estranged oldest brother. And of course, Matthias hadn't made things easy for anyone, as usual. If Judge Piper hadn't shown up, I'm not sure how she'd've been able to handle things.

Shaking my head, I finally slip out of the room. Sama certainly doesn't need any more grief as it is, and she'd likely be traumatized to see me this early in the morning.

She especially didn't need to see me standing in her room, hunting through my purse for my cigarettes, my clothes all wrinkled and my hair sticking up all over the place.

Poor dear was having enough trouble getting through eighth grade math, last Martha and I talked.

I walk down to the living room, where Matthias, Asher, and Judge Piper are all awake. None of the three men seem willing to do much more than sit there and stare off into space.

At least they're quiet now.

Sama'd only really started crying when Matthias and Judge Piper started arguing with each other.

I'm understanding, I truly am; Judge Piper suffers, much as I do; not being able to have children as I am, I recognize the pain of lost dreams in others. I knew he and

Martha had been dating privately for a while now, but they'd been hoping to make it public when Asher and Matthias came home.

Assuming they believed the boys could handle the truth, anyway.

Before, I hadn't had a doubt Asher could, but looking at them now, I might've gotten my guesstimates mixed up.

Asher's lower lip is quivering as he just blankly looks around the room, while Matthias is angrily scowling at Judge Piper in between looking down at his phone.

Boys and their toys …

I bite back a small sigh and put on a polite expression. I can't seem to smile, but I do try to make sure they see I am here to help.

"Morning, everyone," I murmur carefully. They nod toward me, just as polite, before I focus on Judge Piper. "Any updates?"

He shakes his head. "Nothing yet."

"Asher and I are the ones who'll get the reports," Matthias says in a sharp, disdainful tone. "Not you."

"If there's been any foul play, I'll be able to see them myself," Judge Piper reminds him. "Especially if we have to go to court over her death."

"I thought judges needed to recuse themselves in cases that affect their personal judgment."

"Matthias." I cross my arms. "Did you forget your manners?"

He's a little shocked at my shaming, but he looks back down at his phone with a glum expression on his face. "No, ma'am."

"Then please honor your mother and act like it," I insist.

From his angry expression, I might as well've been talking to a wall, and a retarded one at that.

"I'm going home to see to my Donnie," I say. "But if you need anything, please let me know right away."

"There's nothing you can do," Matthias says, reminding me more of Donnie in that moment than I would've liked.

"I know," I agree in a bitter tone. "But if Sama needs me, just call and I'll come on over."

At Sama's name, Asher straightens in his seat. "Don't worry, Mrs. Hennessey, I'll take care of her," he says. He looks down at the floor again. "I've been away for the last couple years, but I'm almost finished with my degree. Once I'm done, I'll move back here so she can finish school here."

"Well, that's mighty sweet of you, Asher." I smile at him. "Your mama would be proud."

"Well, that's good. I've got to get back to Nashville. I can't take her with me." Matthias runs a hand through his hair, clearly relieved he didn't have to worry about his younger sibling.

Half-sibling.

Mentally, I correct myself; Martha wouldn't have liked me saying the truth aloud.

Judge Piper clears his throat. "I would be honored to help you get settled, Asher," he says. "Martha and I are … were … very close, and Sama is comfortable with me."

"Well, she should be, considering you're her father," Matthias snaps.

Judge Piper sighs and looks over at me, but I only shrug and shake my head.

Martha had never said much regarding Sama; all I know is that one day she'd come home from a chef's conference and announced in a state of shock that she was pregnant.

And then, after that, everything changed. Once Sama was born, it was glaringly obvious Martha's husband, Joe, wasn't the father. He was livid about her affair, and so he left Martha. The community quietly pulled back from ordering from her catering company.

I heard the rumors, even though I never pressed Martha myself. We'd been friends and neighbors for a long time, and I could see the whole thing clearly traumatized her, and no good friend wants to press salt into open wounds.

Even a decade later, all she would say was she'd signed an NDA with Sama's biological father. In exchange, she'd been paid for her silence, and she'd given her word that she wouldn't bother him for more money or go to the press.

Despite how things looked, I knew Martha was a good woman, and she kept her word. Though I'd've been willing to gamble quite a bit she'd told Judge Piper the truth at some point.

Unlike Matthias, I don't think the judge is Sama's father.

If Sama was his, he would've admitted it, especially with all that's happened.

"How is Sama, Edith?" Judge Piper asks. His tone is gentle and fatherly enough for me to give him another small smile.

"Right now, she's still snoring away," I say. "She doesn't sleep so easily, so let the poor thing stay in bed as long as she needs to."

He nods as Asher stands up. "I'll start fixing breakfast for her."

"No need." A small, reedy voice speaks up from the kitchen. We all turn to see Pamela, Asher's girlfriend, mixing up something in a bowl. "I thought it might be good to make some eggs."

I notice there's no engagement ring on her finger, and I make a mental note to make sure Asher gets it; Martha'd shown me where she'd put it up for him, on the bookshelf in her bedroom, and he ought to have it even if she's gone now.

"I'm not hungry." Matthias rolls his eyes and looks back at his phone.

Some part of me wants to slap him. But the nice, church-going, Southern-hospitality part of me is in control this morning, as any proper lady would have it.

"That's very kind of you, Patricia," Judge Piper murmurs agreeably.

Pamela blushes, but stands up straight and squares her shoulders. "It's Pamela."

"My apologies." The judge doesn't seem truly repentant, any more than he has to be, but at least he's going through the motions.

Sometimes the motions are all we have until we can find something solid to land on.

I can't express it aloud, but in light of Matthias's carelessness and selfish attitude, I am deeply grateful to have the judge here.

It's nice to see some maturity around here.

I curl my fingers more tightly around my purse again, still longing for another cigarette. "I'm going to go home and check on my Donnie," I say again. "Please let me know if you need me."

"Thank you," Judge Piper says. "But Asher and I can get along for now. Sama might need you later, and then I'll call you."

"Number's on the fridge."

Ever since Asher went off to college, me and Clarice Youngblood had been Martha's closest friends, and we'd been entrusted with emergency contact status if Martha ever needed us.

I don't need to tell them that. Sama will likely be able to do that herself when she wakes up, assuming she'll be able to think clearly at all.

The poor dear. Bless her heart.

I'm only two steps out the door when I stop and pull out my cigarettes.

I'd told Judge Piper the truth, that Sama had slept poorly. But I've neglected to let myself properly feel all the aches and pains I've endured sleeping in that small rocking chair in her room until just this moment, and now I feel like every body part is in full, angry rebellion.

And then, I'm struggling with my own grief and disbelief at Martha's passing.

The flame from my lighter is shaking as I finally light the cigarette and put it to my lips.

I breath in the ash and fire like it's a lifeline, and perhaps this morning it is. I breathe out the smoke too quickly and nearly cough, but I keep quiet.

I don't want to disturb the others.

"Edith?"

Judge Piper appears just behind me, and I finally cough, caught off guard. He's a bigger man, but still graceful, and I hadn't heard his approach.

I feel more than graceless as I finish my racked coughing. "Yes, sir?"

"I wanted to thank you again." He glances back toward the house with a telling expression. "There aren't a lot of people who would step up to do so."

"It seems Asher will," I say. "I know he's likely in shock, but he was always a sweet boy. Too softhearted and sentimental for his own good at times."

"Yes, it seems he got all of Martha's goodness."

The slight, silent jab at Matthias doesn't surprise me.

"I'm sure Matthias will come around," I say carefully. "He was polite to me yesterday. I saw him arrive and spoke to him while Martha finished up talking with Orpah."

"Orpah?" The judge's eyebrows raise in surprise, and then narrow in suspicion. "What was she doing here?"

"Something about the pie festival, I think." I frown, trying to remember what Martha had told me before.

"I heard the rumor that Martha was going to enter this year." Judge Piper frowns. "Was Orpah here for an interview?"

"Oh, who knows?" I wave my hand dismissively. "I'm more likely to think Orpah was worried she'd lose if Martha entered and she came over here to stop her."

"Well, Martha is—was—the best chef I'd ever known." Judge Piper's eyes mist over. "I've loved her and her pies for years now. She would win the pie contest in a heartbeat."

"Of course, she would!" My eyes fill with tears. "You and Garland and Mayor Bottoms would all vote for her for sure."

"Orpah wouldn't be able to show her face on her TV show for weeks," Judge Piper agrees with a small chuckle.

"Martha would like that." I'm crying as we laugh, and I almost drop my cigarette at the image of Orpah Abraham getting humiliated. After some of the stories I've heard about her show, I'd say she'd earned it, though I don't take pride in another's fall. "I'm not sure what Orpah wanted, but she left in a huff after Matthias arrived."

"Did you see Martha?"

"She didn't come out, but I saw Matthias," I say. "He seemed nervous to see her again. She figured he would be, you know. So much trouble in their past."

"Yes, I know."

It's the odd expression on his face and the gleam in his eye that makes me feel worried. I grip my cigarette more tightly as I dare myself to ask the question suddenly raging inside of me. "You don't think Matthias did something, do you?"

My voice is barely a whisper, but Judge Piper doesn't move.

His silence is all the answer I need. For a long moment, we stand there, with smoke billowing out of my cigarette.

"He got some money from her," Judge Piper finally says. "A big check, too. She died right after he came home. And he has a history with drugs, Edith."

"But not hard drugs, or murder," I object.

"He wants to get her funeral wrapped up quickly, and he wants to leave Fairmont as soon as possible."

"Well, he's probably grieving. And he's always wanted to get away from here. Remember after Joe left Martha?"

Judge Piper doesn't seem to remember who Joe is for a long moment, and then he only sighs. "The whole situation is still suspicious," he says. "Maybe Orpah will answer some of our questions."

"The autopsy reports will come later. And I'm sure Officer McCain will have something for you, too."

Judge Piper nods politely, but I can see he's still troubled.

"Anyway, you ought to focus on Asher and Sama more than Matthias," I say. "Martha told me Asher was going to propose to his girlfriend. Can you imagine how terrible he feels now that she's not going to be at his wedding?"

Martha, Clarice, and I had just talked on Sunday at one of our brunches about Asher's plan to marry Pamela. We hadn't talked much about Matthias, other than to wonder if he would come home for the wedding if we could convince Asher to hold it here.

"And poor Sama," I add, recalling my own aching body. "She's absolutely devastated. I can't imagine how bad it'll be if Martha was murdered after all. And to think Matthias had something to do with it? It's all just so sad."

"The truth is often sad," Judge Piper agrees wisely. "But I still want to uncover it—and I want to arrest and sentence the responsible party. It's the one thing I can do for Martha. And for Sama, too."

"That's not the only thing you can do for that poor girl." I drop the cigarette and smother the flame into the ground. "You can find her father."

Judge Piper goes still, too shocked and angry and upset and sad to do much more than try to keep it all together.

"Martha didn't want Sama's father in her life," he finally says.

"What about Joe?" I ask.

"What about him?"

"Well, he might be a concern, since Sama is still only fifteen and they might want to question him about custody. Do you know if Martha had drawn up a will?"

There's a million more questions that need answered, and I'm more than ready to be Sama's advocate if needed.

But, of course, before the judge can say anything, Donnie opens the window at the side of our house.

"Edith, what the hell's keeping you?"

I bite back a groan as I nod politely at Judge Piper. "I'm sorry, but I do need to go now. Please let me know if I can help in some other way."

"There's not much you can do for Martha now," Judge Piper says glumly. "But I'll let you know. Thanks."

There's something about the way he says it that reminds me of Donnie.

Fundamentally, I know that's the truth; Martha's dead, and only the good Lord has power over death. But it is so hard to accept I just can't do *anything*.

Surely, there's something I can do to honor my best friend.

Isn't there?

"I don't know," I murmur to myself, as I walk into the door of my house. Already I'm on the verge of tears again, and it doesn't help that when I open the door, I knock over a small pile of my old realtor yard signs.

I'm suddenly ready to scream.

Instead, I calmly, calmly kneel down and pick up the fallen items.

"You don't know what?" Donnie leans back in his recliner and burps. Before I can answer, he looks down at the mess I'd inadvertently made and scoffs. "Never mind. You'd have an easier time telling me what you do know."

Despite his jab, I'm a little grateful. My sudden flare of anger and injustice helps me keep my tears locked in place, and I muster the energy to straighten up, brush off my dress with some dignity, and clear my throat.

"I was just thinking that there's not much I can do for Martha," I explain.

Last night, I'd managed to tell Donnie what'd happened a little before I'd gone back to Martha's house, but it's as clear as day from the look on his face he doesn't care much.

"Well, people die pretty regularly," he says, only somewhat kindly.

"True." I don't dare roll my eyes at him, even though I wish, futilely, that he was just a bit more gentle.

I'm no fool, though.

Donnie had once been a career infantry man. On his last tour, fifteen or so years ago now, he'd gotten a busted-up knee along with several other burns and cuts and scrapes, thanks to a shrapnel grenade thrown by an enemy fighter.

It'd scarred him for life in more than one way.

Throughout our years together, I was able to piece the story together from his drunken rants and half-slumbering stupors. Donnie had returned fire to "kill the bastard," and he'd succeeded.

But when he went to inspect his kill, he saw it was only a child, fighting in a war he didn't understand past the propaganda. The young boy died for reasons he couldn't even likely articulate, yet he'd been shot brutally and repeatedly.

He doesn't say it, but I think he's relieved we couldn't have kids—although it's also one of the reasons he was upset we didn't, too.

Grief is a strange thing, that's for sure.

When I try to comfort him, he only pushes me away and reminds me I've failed spectacularly in my life, too, from being unable to have children to my realtor career to my attempts to learn photography and become a reporter, and many of my various other attempts at careers and hobbies.

"Judge Piper said he'll let me know if Sama needs any help. Poor girl's lost her mother and her whole life is about to change."

Donnie shrugs. "Change is a part of life. You adapt or you die. And sometimes even if you adapt, you die."

I glance over at my realtor signs. I remember how much money, time, effort, and soul went into my work, only to have it all flatten and fold.

I clear my throat. "Well, she's only fifteen."

"So was I, when I signed up to go to war," Donnie snaps back.

I cross my arms; I happen to know when Donnie was nineteen, he'd gone into the army, and it was only because he couldn't afford college.

"I'd still like to do something, if I can," I say, keeping my tone light. "I just can't think of a suitable gift or tribute or something."

"If you ask me, it's best if you just keep your nose out of everything," Donnie says. "'Specially with her kids at home now. Matthias ain't nobody to cross, from what you've heard from Clarice and them. And Judge Piper's there, too. He'll be eager for blood himself now that Martha's dead."

Sometimes I wonder how Donnie knows what's going on so well; I swear the man must have ears that can hear a turtle snoring two towns over.

"Are you going to get breakfast soon?" Donnie asks, picking up the television remote. "I'm hungry."

I wait for him to add his usual, "It's the one thing you do right around here," and I'm a little surprised when he doesn't say it.

"What would you like, hun?" I ask.

"Bacon and eggs, and grits, too, if we've got 'em."

"Alright. I'll get it."

I can hear how half-hearted his "Thank you," is as I open the fridge.

I pull out the butter and bacon, and I get them started in the frying pan while I go to get the eggs.

When I pull them out, I notice the carton's almost empty. Donnie likes his eggs, and he could easily go through four or five dozen every week. I move the one carton to the side to see if there's another one.

That's when I see it, and everything goes still.

There's a small pie box in the back. Martha had made both me and Clarice a special pie this past week; she'd been intent on practicing for the Pie Festival, or so she'd said at our last Sunday brunch.

I take out the box carefully, almost reverently, as an idea starts to take hold inside of me.

I'd brought it home for Donnie, saving some by only the sheerest force of will. He'd refused, of course, probably knowing I'd feel bad, but now I was glad he'd refused.

"Where are my eggs?" Donnie yells from the other room.

"Look, Donnie," I say, walking out to show him. "Martha gave me a pie the other day. I still have half left."

He sniffs loudly. "So? I said I wanted bacon and eggs, and grits, too. Not pie."

"Maybe I should take it to Sama, or … " I pause carefully. "Or maybe I could enter it in the Pie Festival contest. Don't you think Martha would like that?"

"She's dead, Edith; she probably don't really care about the contest. And anyway, you'd need a full pie to qualify. What are you going to do? Bake half of another pie for her?"

The pie in my hands warms with my sudden fury. "I could make a good one, if I had to."

I look down at the open pie box, eying Martha's pie carefully. This one she'd made for me was lemon meringue.

I've never made one, but surely it can't be that hard … can it?

"Remember the last time you wanted to try something that was supposedly easy?" Donnie gestures to the far corner of the room, where my realtor signs and pamphlets and business cards are all stacked up.

"I've done some fine work in the past," I argue, straightening my shoulders. "And I could've expanded my business, if I didn't need to come home and cater to your lazy ass so much."

"I got a busted knee defending democracy. And do I need to remind you that it's only because of my stipend we were able to pay off the debts from your licensing, your profile photos, your website-do-hicky, and all that gas you used showing houses? Face it, you've sunk more money into your job than you've gotten out of it. And that's just from your realtor business. What about all the other things you've bailed out on?"

"I bailed out on them because of you!" I shout back, surprised my long-simmering anger had broken through my politeness. "You always needed me home for dinner and you didn't like if I left any time before nine in the morning."

"Well, they weren't good jobs for you anyways," he argues. "You were miserable driving around that much, you hated dealing with the lawyers, and all your clients annoyed you, and the computer stuff was too hard for you to learn."

Donnie lists out my various complaints over the years, along with some of the higher bills and costs and expenditures I've used. All I can do is stand there, shocked and angry beyond words.

"Face it," Donnie finally says. "You're not your friends. Martha had her catering business, and Clarice has been her husband's secretary for so long I can't remember if she had the job first or if she was his wife before that. They both felt they needed a job to feel good about themselves. But you? You're my wife, and that's all I need you to be. And you don't have to prove yourself to me or anyone else. You fail at everything else."

The pan on the stove starts to crackle from the heat, and before Donnie's meal can get burned, I quietly excuse myself.

Once I'm back in the kitchen, I put the pie box back in the fridge, full of sadness and profound defeat. My tears of grief over Martha's death turn into tears of self-pity and self-loathing.

It takes me a few moments to calm down.

I know there's nothing to be done about Martha, and there's nothing to be done about me and my situation, neither.

A small, rueful smirk curls on my lips.

Donnie's defeatism has finally sunk into me, I guess.

Once I've composed myself, I serve Donnie his food, and as he's eating and mindlessly watching TV, I quietly head out to smoke again.

I step onto my porch; at once, I catch sight of Asher. He's a little more put together this time. He's changed his clothes, and he's walking out to his car.

Judge Piper's Cadillac is missing from the driveway now, and I hope to God he's gone to find some answers for all of us. Meanwhile Matthias' old, beat-up car is still parked, too. Asher's car is respectable but modest, and I feel sad again, knowing that Martha will never see him married now.

As I watch him, he opens the back door to the car and pulls out several apples. I wonder if he'd brought some for Sama; she always loved her mama's apple pie—pie she'll never have, ever again.

Bless their hearts.

I don't know what compels me to move forward, but I call his name.

"Asher."

The sad expression on Asher's face is nearly unbearable as he looks at me. I walk over to him, eager to comfort him, and I watch as his nose sniffles at my cigarette smoke.

I quickly put it out. Donnie says he's allergic to the smoke, but I don't believe him. Asher, on the other hand, seems a lot more delicate.

"I almost forgot earlier," I say. "I wanted to tell you that Martha and I had talked a few times about your wedding plans."

He shakes his head. "It doesn't mean much right now, Mrs. Hennessey."

I don't know why I feel irritated.

Can't he see I'm trying to help him?

"Nonsense," I say lightly. "I know a lot of things have happened, but I know where Martha kept her ring. She wants … I mean, she wanted you to have it for Pamela."

Asher hesitates again, and immediately, I push forward. "I know there's not a lot I can do to help, and while you probably don't want to propose right now, I'd like to make sure it gets to you. For when you're ready."

He says nothing, but only looks back at the house. "I'm not sure Pamela would want that."

"Well, I know the timing's uncertain, but it's still a nice gesture, to give her your mama's ring." I put my hand on his arm and start tugging him after me. "Come on. Let me get it for you, and you can make new plans to surprise Pamela when you're ready."

Asher pauses, but he is too polite; he tepidly nods in agreement.

Triumphantly, I help take in the rest of his apples, and once they're put away, I lead the way to Martha's room.

The room feels empty of her presence already. It's clean and neat, and I wonder if she'd tidied it up extra-special, probably since Matthias was coming to visit her. She wanted to make him feel proud, even if she lived in a poor town. I often envied

her talent for cleaning when she was nervous; I can't say I clean unless I'm obligated to, and even then, it's definitely a chore.

Asher pauses at the doorway, unnerved, but I saunter on determinedly.

Martha's bookshelf is stuffed full of her cookbooks, travel journals, and business books. She was a woman who'd traveled a lot in her life, but eventually, she'd chosen to come back home. She told me once it was time to leave her wings behind and water her roots, and I just loved that she'd said it, just like that.

There were other little trinkets on her shelves: an old ashtray full of seashells, a small analog alarm clock, a few framed pictures, including one of Martha holding up a pie, and several smaller items like buttons, safety pins, and some pieces of jewelry.

Tucked in the middle of the top shelf is a black velvet ring box, and I can feel my eyes light up in excitement as I reach up and grab it.

"Here you go," I say, handing the box to Asher with pride.

Asher handles the box carefully, almost like he's afraid it'll turn into a snake and bite him.

"Thanks, Mrs. Hennessey," he mutters, and for the first time, I realize he may not be as eager to marry Pamela as I'd thought. "Excuse me. I'll go put this in my suitcase."

He leaves the room rather abruptly, and I'm left alone.

Well, I did something helpful. So there's that.

I turn to face the photo of Martha. "I'm sorry you're gone," I whisper. "But I'll do my best to watch over them and help as I can. I only wish there was something I could do for you."

Martha's bright smile seems to wink at me, even if the pie in her hands seems more eager to mock me.

That's when I look behind the picture and see an old, worn out book labeled "Family Recipes."

Martha's recipes.

Burning, curious temptation strikes me harder than I've ever felt, and I can't do anything but succumb to the book's siren call of doom.

Quickly, I peek out into the hallway.

No one is coming. No one is around.

My fingers carefully grab hold of the book.

Once I open it, I see a plethora of papers; some sheets are falling out, some are faded, and others are torn. But all of them are marked with Martha's precise handwriting.

Including a folded one, right on top—a recently consulted recipe for lemon meringue pie.

My earlier idea comes back to me.

I think of how Martha couldn't stand Orpah, and how Martha's family and friends and loved ones would never get to taste her pies ever again.

I think of Donnie, and how he wouldn't help me.

It's at the thought of Donnie that I grab the recipe and put the book back.

I look back at the photo. "I'll give it back when I'm done," I tell her. "I promise. You were the real Pie Queen around here, and you deserve to unseat Orpah."

The picture says nothing back to me, but I nod.

This is something I can do.

This is something I have to do.

For Martha, I silently clarify to myself. *This is something I can do for Martha.*

I glance at the clock next to her seashells.

If I hurry.

I slide out of the house, silent as ever, and head back home. No one stops me, no one says anything—no one suspects anything.

When I arrive home, Donnie's asleep in his recliner, while the news is on.

As he snores away, I call Clarice, and I ask her for a few favors. After that, I write a note to Donnie telling him I went shopping for more eggs—technically not a lie—and head out to the store, and then Clarice's house.

I'm barely breathing as I drive. All I can think is *"Don't mess this up, Edith"* over and over again.

"Edith!" Clarice meets me in her driveway as I pull up. I'm barely out of my car as she pulls me into a hug.

"I was hoping the rumors weren't true," she says into my shoulder.

"I'm sorry they're not," I whisper back as I hug her. "Martha was such a good friend."

For a few moments, we share a good cry; we both need it, and we both know we do. That's why we're friends, even if we're a bit of an odd pairing standing next to each other.

Clarice is half a foot shorter than me, with brightly dyed hair that's half-grown out. She's curled it this morning, letting it warmly clash with her patterned silk scarf. Her nails are freshly done as she takes my arm and pulls me into her house. Everything about her seems to clash against my drab housedress, graying hair, and pearl necklace.

"So, tell me why you need my help entering the pie contest," Clarice says. "You know the deadline isn't until six tonight. That's plenty of time for you to bake a pie."

"I know that," I say. "But I'm hoping that you'll cover for me in a few ways."

I explain to her what had happened: Finding Martha's half a pie in my fridge, discovering the recipe in Martha's bedroom, and just knowing how much Martha would love to put Orpah in her place, if only once.

"I see," Clarice says. "Hmm."

"Well? What do you think of my plan?" I ask. "Does it make sense? Or am I just crazy?"

"Just cause something's sensible doesn't mean it's not crazy," Clarice says. "But I think Martha would love it, personally. She always did her best to avoid Orpah like the plague."

"You're okay with telling the judges that we'll use the pie Martha gave us on Sunday?"

"Sure, no problem there."

"And … " My cheeks heat as I pull out the groceries I'd purchased earlier. "You're okay with me baking it here?"

Clarice gives me a knowing glare. "Of course. Wouldn't want Donnie to blow out his other knee. Goodness knows he'd probably throw out his back trying to kick you out of the house for going against his word."

"My Donnie's never hurt me."

Clarice rolls her eyes. "Physically."

"And he didn't tell me *not* to bake a pie," I say, trying not to slip back into my self-pity. "He just said I wouldn't be able to, most likely."

"Whatever, hun. You just get to baking. I'll get to the festival and put Martha's name on the list."

I pause for a moment. "Do you really think I can do this, Clarice? Martha was such a good baker, and it seems like I'm just good at failing."

"Oh, pssh. Stop listening to Donnie like that." Clarice takes my hand. "First, let me remind you that Donnie's failed at his own life plenty of times. And while you might've had your own setbacks, you don't just roll over and give up. You get back up. That takes courage, Edith. Real courage. Tell me, when was the last time Donnie ever tried something new? Man can't even cook his own meals, for goodness' sakes."

"Well, he is the breadwinner of our family," I murmur, remembering Donnie's words from earlier. "He makes more money with his pension than I make doing anything else."

"Oh, please," Clarice scoffs. "Money isn't everything. Now, let me also remind you that our dear friend, Martha Davidson, said many times that love was her secret ingredient. What could be more loving them two of her friends scheming to win her the title of Pie Queen out from the likes of someone like Orpah Abraham? You just do your best, darling, and love and God's sense of divine humor will take care of the rest."

"Maybe." I give her my best smile, and I think she believes me.

I'm thankful for her support, truly I am, but I'm even more grateful when Clarice leaves me alone in the kitchen.

Making a pie—especially one as good as Martha's—is more difficult than I'd thought. I follow the recipe, right down to dotting all the i's and crossing all the t's, but it takes me three times as long as it should've.

The crust is too thin at first, and then it's too fat; the meringue is fluffier than a cloud, and by the time the filling is sifted properly, I feel like an Alaskan gold digger down on the beach.

All the while, I'm fighting off Donnie's perpetual discouragement inside my mind, telling me that I'm just going to fail.

Clarice encourages me, but when she heads out to register Martha for the contest, I'm left all alone.

Tears streak down my cheeks and fall into the lemon filling while I scoop out the fluffy whipped meringue from Clarice's mixing bowl.

"Please, God." I quietly pray as I scoop and sculpt the white topping using a spatula and a kitchen torch. "For Martha's sake, and mine, too, please don't let me fail."

LEMON ICEBOX PIE WITH MERINGUE

A BANKER FAMILY RECIPE

From the kitchen of Mary Banker and her daughters, Helen and Dale

LEMON ICEBOX PIE WITH MERINGUE

Ingredients:

3 eggs, separated

1 can condensed milk

½ cup fresh lemon juice (3 lemons)

¼ TSP cream of tartar

$1/_3$ cup sugar

1 baked pie shell or graham

cracker crust

Mix egg yolks (beaten) with condensed milk and lemon juice.

Pour into pie shell.

Beat 3 chilled egg whites with cream of tartar. Gradually add sugar a little at a time and beat until stiff peaks form. Spread over pie to edges (seal edges so meringue doesn't shrink).

Make "peaks" on meringue top.

Bake at 350° for 12-15 minutes or until browned on top.

Cool pie and then chill.

from
DALE BANKER

"This was Mary Banker's recipe in the 50's, and she was my mother. My older sister (18 months older) and I loved to bake when we were teenagers. We asked mom if we could make the pie and she would get us the ingredients.

"We also loved to bake brownies, German Chocolate Cake, and make fudge. Sometimes we gave fudge and brownies away, but we always kept the lemon pie for ourselves. Sometimes you just have to have pie!!!!!!!"

NO MORE MISS NICE PIE

AN AMBITIOUS WOMAN FACES OPPOSITION

Life of Pies, #5

C. S. Johnson

CHAPTER FIVE
Orpah Abraham

The morning is as busy as usual, and, not for the first time, that means I'm busier than usual, too.

But there's never really time for a vacation when you're the queen of your own media empire.

Oh, sure, I can schedule a couple of weeks of re-runs for my top-rated television show in between breaks, and I can jettison away when a famous movie star or politician invites me to one of their prestigious parties or fundraisers.

But it's important to keep going, especially if you're going to keep people on their toes.

And that's the way I prefer them.

A leader has to keep moving; that's how you remain the queen, after all. If you settle down for too long, they might start to question why they're excited to see you in the first place.

I breathe in deeply, repeating my successful thinking mantras silently to myself.

I deserve this.

I am a winner.

I will do whatever it takes.

No one can stop me—

"Ouch!" I open my eyes, frowning even more when I feel my facial mask start to crack. I look down at the nail technician who's halfway through my strawberry-themed pedicure. "Yamiko, watch my cuticles, would you? They're tender."

"Sorry, Miss Abraham."

Yamiko's voice is contrite and grating at the same time. She's a nobody, someone without power and without purpose, aside from when she serves me—and we both know it.

So, I decide to be understanding and gracious. If she's nothing, it's nothing for me to forgive her.

I give her my sweetest, most glowing smile, if only because we're in a public TV station, in a large dressing room, and others are watching. Who knows if there's an undercover journalist here or not these days?

"I'm sorry, too," I tell her, leaving out the part that I have to hire incompetent staff. "But I just stubbed that poor toe just the other day. I suppose I forgot to remind you?"

"No, ma'am." She doesn't seem as penitent as before. She looked over at her other Japanese-Korean teammates and then the group of ladies working on my hair. "You also told us you had special cream—"

"Yes, thank you so much." I interrupt her smoothly, before she can announce to the whole room about my bad case of foot fungus.

When you're famous, people especially love it when you suffer. But if you're like me, you know you don't even have to be famous for people to enjoy that.

My smile remains unabated as I look down at Yamiko. "I'm glad you'll be extra careful from now on, Yamiko. I know I can count on Dreamy Nails to give me their best. I'm looking forward to giving it a glowing review on my show one day."

Yamiko quickly nods, once more grateful I'm not going to fire her and the rest of her team and drag her business through the media mud.

I'm just happy when she gets back to work.

I'm further happy when the women working on my hair start braiding extra-gently, too.

As much as I'm excited for my thicker cornrow braids, I know I definitely need my strawberry-colored toes for today's broadcast from the Fairmont Spring Festival as I announce what kind of pie I'm going to enter into the contest this year.

Assuming I enter at all.

The thought slips silently into my mind and sends a shiver down my spine. I close my eyes against the sudden chill.

With considerable effort, I push it away and once more repeat my inner mantras to myself.

I deserve this.

I am a winner.

I will do whatever it takes.

No one can stop me.

I open my eyes, letting my nerves relax. No one will stop me, no matter what.

I'd suffered my entire life. A million moments of rejection, hate, dismissiveness, and ridicule all flowed through me like a warming balm.

The men who'd said I was "too dark," "too fat," "too ugly."

The women who'd said the gap in my teeth was "unsightly, distracting," and "large enough to floss with a bath towel."

My rivals in school who'd said I'd "never make it."

My political enemies, who constantly dismissed me as "too naïve," "too inexperienced," and "not particularly talented."

Even my own grandmother, who'd raised me, saying I was "too proud to learn how to fail," and the main reason I wasn't married was because I was "too ambitious."

My eyes are watering now, with angry tears.

"Can you please go just a bit more carefully, Angie?" I turn my head just slightly to see if I can catch the gaze of my lead hairdresser.

"Sure thing, Miss Abraham," she replies.

Her voice is much more rich and soothing than Yamiko's, I notice. I smile again. "Thank you."

"Miss Orpah?"

My personal assistant—Shirley? Sheryl? Sherry? I'm pretty sure it's Sherry—appears in front of me with her clipboard ready.

"Ah, there you are," I say. I pretend to look her over, glad to see that she did have a nametag on that said "Sherry" in bright red lettering. "How are we doing? Everything is on schedule?"

"Yes, ma'am." Sherry held up her clipboard and pulled out her phone. "11Alive News is getting our car ready so they can interview you right as you arrive at the festival and officially sign your ballot for the Pie Queen Contest. Not that you need to worry about that, of course. They might as well hand you the trophy while you're at it."

"Oh, yes," I agree with a congenial laugh. "Hold up my mirror and let me see how progress is going."

Sherry complies at once, and I'm glad I managed to find a good worker intent on pleasing me. They aren't hard to find, now that I'm a household name and a reputable brand, but back when I started my political campaigns, no one seemed willing to believe that I, the "sassy, articulate black lady" could win. And when I didn't, it was clear there was still plenty of racism out there I would have to fight.

So that's exactly what I set out to do.

Sherry holds up the mirror and I examine myself carefully.

My makeup needs refreshed, but I have my thicker cornrows flowing down into dark, ebony curls; it gives me a cute, fun look, which is always a bit dangerous in professional circles. But this is for the Fairmont Spring Festival, and it's supposed to be fun. My nails are bright red with little green jewels at the cuticles, and my outfit is a splash of red, purple, and black colors set in a batik style.

"One more layer of makeup, and then I'll be all ready," I say to Sherry. "And then I need my jewelry. Also, were we able to get a poodle for today's broadcast?"

"No, they didn't have any at the local pet shop," Sherry replies. "But maybe we could try a pet shelter. That's the kind of business that would appreciate us more, and we could talk about pet fostering on TV. That way if it came out that you don't actually own the dog, it wouldn't be something people could fixate on. You haven't mentioned your charity work in a while."

My fingers tingle and twitch in involuntary disgust. If I wanted to provide an update on my charity work, I'd have to call Omar. My brother wasn't my favorite person by a longshot. Buying him a private house in the Hamptons was my own form of charity, even if it was to myself. Keeping him there meant I didn't have to deal with him more than I needed to.

But I do need to talk to him.

Sherry has a point.

"Well, I wanted a poodle. But if you can find a poodle mix, we can do that instead," I say instead, focusing more on the part of the problem I can control.

Besides, I want a poodle for my performance today. And it's important to tell people what you want, and then be reasonable if you can't get it.

No one wants to follow a lunatic, even if you always want your fans to be fanatics.

All the crazy should be on one side—the side you can arrest, if it's needed.

Sherry nods in understanding, but I can tell she's worried as she heads off to make some calls.

I can't really be too bothered by it. I don't have the time.

After a few more fix-ups, I'm shinier than a new penny, and I'm ready to go.

~

The ride over to the Fairmont Spring Festival is a short one; it's really in the heart of downtown, and downtown in small town like Fairmont is only ever twenty minutes away with traffic.

I try to hide my disdain as we pass through the town. It's so old-fashioned; I honestly only really ever come here for one thing, and thirteen years ago, the Pie Festival was something that would get me noticed on the political spectrum. I got a lot of praise from the right people with my comments of how not all women had to stay home and make pies, but it would be a shame for someone like me not to celebrate great pies anyway.

I received a lot of insults for that one, too; some people called me fat, while others said I was misogynistic and self-hating. But even bad media is good for your business and its reputation.

The chill I felt earlier slivers down my back again as I remember I still need to get my pie plans in order.

This year is going to be different, that's for sure.

"Can you turn the radio on?" I ask, fanning myself as I try to hide my discomfort.

I could've really used that loaner dog to distract me.

Sherry hurried to make me happy again, nudging our chauffeur.

"—sad news to report this week as longtime local resident, Martha Davidson, passed away this week—"

I swallow my smile at the news.

Good. She's dead.

"Oh, no." The driver shakes his head, pulling off his cap and wiping his face. "That's terrible news. My mama loved Mrs. Martha's cooking."

"I'm sure another company will be along to help fill the void in the catering business," I say. "In fact, Sherry, let's make a note. Perhaps I can find someone who can set up shop here. I was just thinking this week that we need to branch out into some kind of food marketing. 'Orpah's Originals,' or something like that. It'll go well with my Powerhouse Figure Weight Loss Coffee blend."

"Oh, that sounds great," Sherry agrees. She holds up her own thermos. "Ever since you featured it on your show last month, I've been drinking it non-stop and I've lost four pounds. If you're going in the healthy food business, I'll be your first customer."

Sherry goes on prattling about her plans to snag a date for her sister's upcoming wedding, and while I'm pretending to care about her personal life, I notice the driver just rolls his eyes.

"Excuse me, sir? What's the problem?" I ask. "Did I offend you somehow, trying to be helpful?"

"No ma'am," he says. "Just focusing on the traffic here."

"There's barely any traffic," I point out, trying my best to keep my polite face on. It's so tempting to remind him his job is in my hands, and so is his company's existence. I'd spent the last years building up myself as a media queen, and I wasn't about to excuse his rudeness. "Why don't you tell me what you're really annoyed with?"

"Nothing. It's nothing." He shrugs, but Sherry frowns at him, while I fold my hands over my chest. Both of us wait for him to explain himself.

Finally, he rolls his eyes again. "Fine. Miss Martha's more than just her job. I'm sure lots of her friends and family will be upset. It's a shame she passed."

I wrinkle my nose disdainfully, and then let out a huff. "Well, I can't help with that. But I can help put Fairmont on the map with some kind of catering business, and I just happen to have several binders full of references—references that can help your community."

"No disrespect toward you, Miss Abraham," he grumbles. "We're almost there. You'd best get ready to make your entrance."

Sherry looks to me to take her cue, and after a long, thoughtful silence, I finally give her a nod.

I then also give her a silent signal to let her know to leave a terrible review online for the driver's company. Sherry knows what to do at this point; she'll call later and make sure they know I've been gravely insulted, and if we don't get something out of it—some kind of discount or freebie—then we're done with them, and for good.

I can't have people treating me like this.

Once one person starts treating you like this, and you don't stop it, it only gets worse.

It reminds me too much of my past. I think back to the days where I'd be overlooked, ignored, and then demeaned because of how I looked, how much I weighed, or where I'd come from, where I'd gone to school, or what I believed.

Some people may say I'm being a hypocrite for "bullying" other people. But they don't understand; having power and watching other people use theirs is a completely different experience.

When you have power, you have to protect it; to keep it, you have to respect it, and then you have to make sure others do, too. That means there are consequences for people who abuse you and run you over. You can't be sorry about it, either; you're not the one who caused them to disappoint you. Sure, facing consequences isn't fun, but how else are they going to learn?

Sherry has my makeup bag on hand as I step out into the sun and make my way into the Fairmont Spring Festival.

With each step, my unease grows. More and more I think about Martha, and then I think about Omar, and then I look around and think about how I shouldn't be here at all.

Perhaps my driver, as rude and insensitive as he'd been, had a point.

I look down at my strawberry pedicure. The

The Pie Contest is always a festival highlight, but they've made it so you have to walk through the whole park to get to it. They obviously want you to look around and get distracted, and as someone who's in the business of selling things, I can't blame them. There's a lot of money to be made in branded merchandising.

As I walk up, I look to see Mayor Bottoms is already there, sitting behind the Pie Table like some kind of overweight slob of a judge. I don't know how he keeps getting picked as a representative of the community here, except I guess everyone else is too lazy to run against him.

I could run against him and win in a landslide, if I didn't obviously represent the modern era to the hillbillies and regressives in Fairmont.

I am a smart, well-connected, progressive woman, and I aim to rule where I conquer. Mayor Bottoms is a better fit for the town than I am.

My smile is instantaneous as he catches sight of me.

"Hello, Orpah!" he practically cheers as he waddles around the table to come and give me a side-hug. "I'm so glad to see you! I thought you would be here at the start of the festival."

"Oh, I got caught up in meeting with a very famous celebrity over a hush-hush project," I say, giving him a conspiratorial wink. "I'll have to let you know the details once we decide to move forward."

"Ooh, please do." He spends the next several moment fawning over me, complimenting my dress, my hair, and even my strawberry-colored toes.

"Thank you," I say, trying to wave him away. "I've been thinking about my pie for this year."

"Last year, you did a wonderful blueberry crème pie," Mayor Bottoms reminded me. "Sometimes I still wake up dreaming about it. What are you going to make this year?"

"Well, that's the thing," I say carefully. "I've been thinking of not entering this year."

A collective gasp went out from the crowd. Sherry drops my makeup bag in shock, and then she tries to play it cool. She probably thinks I said that in order to gin up more excitement and drama around things this year.

But the moment I said it, I'd felt such peace.

Perhaps this is truly the right thing to do.

I have the perfect excuse for not entering, too. And right now, I have a perfectly captive audience.

I look around again and straighten my shoulders.

"I have been so saddened to hear of the passing of my good friend, Martha Davidson," I say slowly. I'm still trying to get the words to come to me in a way that seems authentic. But this is an impromptu sort of speech, and I need practice if I'm going to sound authentic.

I decide to lean in on the grief aspect. People are more forgiving if you're grieving.

"Anyway, for those of you who didn't know her, she was a very lovely woman," I continue. "She was an inspiration to women everywhere. She was also one of my best friends, especially when it came to baking. Her catering cooking will be greatly missed by the entire community."

There's a thick silence around me as I speak, and I take it to mean I'm doing well. I smile, trying to be sad as I speak again.

"I'm not sure I feel up to making my pie this year, as I put a lot of love into my work, and my heart is just broken this year, knowing I'll never have her cheering me on ever again."

Several of the people are nodding, but some are still in shock.

I'm about to bow out, grateful my plan is working, when a voice calls out from the middle of the crowd.

"You're just scared that she'll actually beat you this year."

The crowd collectively gasps, before it parts down the middle to reveal the speaker.

There, walking toward me, is Clarice Youngblood, one of Martha's real friends. I put my hand on my hip.

"Oh, it's Mrs. Youngblood," I say. "I'm sure you're just as sad as I am at Martha's death."

"I'm sure I'm much more sad than you," Clarice says defiantly. "I have it on good authority you didn't actually like her at all. I'm not sure why Martha never entered the Pie Contest, but I'm willing to believe it was because you threatened her or bribed her."

Another collective gasp went out from the crowd, and I could feel the eyeballs widen as Clarice stood directly in front of me.

"I'm so sorry you're grieving, and you've lost your manners in your sadness," I finally reply, only half as quietly as possible. I want to make sure other people can hear, but I also don't want them to think I'm being mean on purpose. "But Martha and I were good friends."

"If you were really good friends, you'd enter your pie this year," Clarice says. "And then you'll finally know whether or not she was a better pie-maker than you, once and for all."

"Yes, enter, Orpah!" Someone else from the crowd calls out.

"No, she should support Martha," another voice says.

The crowd breaks out in arguments.

This time, I look to Sherry, who's keenly invested in me.

She nods fervently. "No one else has won thirteen times in a row," she whispers. "It'll be historic. And think of the ratings! Perhaps your pie can even be the first 'Orpah Original,' right?"

"But—" I start to tell her it'll look bad if I beat out a dead lady, when I realize what I'm saying. "But we have a problem."

The crowd hushes over again. "What is it?"

"Are you scared?"

"You're not really going to dishonor Martha's memory, are you?"

Sherry steps forward. "People, please! Orpah is very busy, and this is clearly a hard decision for her. Please give her respect."

"Thank you," I say, pleased once more to have such a helpful stooge as my PA. "I was going to say, I know Martha was a very talented pie-maker before she died. But there's no way to know for sure if she was better than me, truly. It's very clear that she can't enter this year's contest."

"Oh, yes she can!" Clarice declares, and then my spine starts to chill over like ice. "As it happens, Martha baked me and Edith a pie yesterday, and we're going to enter it into the contest for her."

"Martha actually made a pie?" Mayor Bottoms is intrigued. "I didn't think she'd ever enter."

"Well, she is," Clarice says. "As long as I have the permission from the judges to sign for her entrance."

I breathe out a sigh of relief. "Well, you can't do that. That's not fair."

"I'm okay with it," Mayor Bottoms says. "I'm sure Judge Piper will be fine with it, too, and we only need a majority vote. Though I'm sure Mr. Morris won't take issue with this situation, either."

I want to punch him, but Clarice only grins at me.

"Well, life isn't fair, Orpah, and neither is death, apparently." Clarice leans in and loses the friendly edge to her voice. "You know as well as I do that Martha might be dead, but even in Heaven, she'll love beating you. And if you don't enter, you'll still be a loser."

The word burns into me bitterly, as I think about how I'd lost my political run years before. I'd been called a loser before, but I was determined not to stay one.

"Fine." My teeth are grinding against each other as I turn to Mayor Bottoms. "I'll enter, too. And I'm going to make a strawberry rhubarb pie."

I'd just talked to my grandmother a few days ago, and she'd mentioned how the strawberry rhubarb pies were selling down at her local shop.

Like hotcakes, she'd said, before laughing hysterically at her own joke.

"Good." Clarice smirks. "I'm glad Martha will get her chance to best you after all."

"You'd best be careful with that tone of yours," I mutter back at her. "I know you work for your husband, but it would be a shame if something happened to his business."

A new voice speaks up behind me. "Is that a proper threat, Orpah?"

My spine is full of electrifying chill as I recognize Judge Piper's voice.

I turned around slowly to give myself a moment to compose myself.

When I face him, I can only bite down on my cheek in frustration. Mayor Bottoms is bit of a clown, but I expect that of a constantly re-elected, unchallenged mayor of a small hick town. But Charles Piper is a refined black man, an imposing figure, well-known and respected in the town. Frankly, I expect better of him. He likely experienced the similar racism I'd faced, and he should've been more eager to be on my side.

Of course, he'd been sweet on Martha Davidson, so he'd been a race-traitor for a long time now. Losing her could be a good thing for him, and I ought to make a nice, polite case for such an outcome.

"Charles," I say with my bright smile on my face again as I hold out my hand for him to shake. "You've gotten here just in time. Mrs. Youngblood here is trying to register Martha for the pie contest."

"She has my permission," Judge Piper says, disappointing me all over again. "I've heard the rumors Martha wanted to enter. I'm happy to support her, even if she's gone."

"Thank you, Judge Piper," Clarice says, beaming with pleasure.

"I think you should resign as judge if you're going to be openly supporting Martha," I say, eager to point out his bias. "How will we know the truth if you're compromised?"

"Martha is gone." Judge Piper looks grim. "She can't bribe me. Or even threaten me. I have a job to do, and I'll see that it gets done. My record speaks for my integrity."

I arch my brow. "Does it?"

He smiles humorlessly. "Of course. If I was truly biased for Martha's sake, I wouldn't have sentenced her oldest son so badly before."

Mayor Bottoms interrupts me. "I'm sure Orpah's just checking to make sure the playing field is fair and level. Can't compete with a ghost too well, can we?"

"True," Judge Piper agrees. "But we can't play fairly with threats, either. And I think that's more Orpah's problem here."

"Well, you would think that," I snap.

"You're right, and your record speaks to that, as well." He steps closer to me, blocking Mayor Bottoms from hearing us. "Martha told me once how you threatened to go after me. I don't know how she managed to stop you from reporting on her son's criminal activity and our relationship, but now that she's gone, I'm happy to set the record straight on that court case. Your threats won't work on me."

"I never threatened her," I insist.

"Yes, but you weren't happy when she told you the truth about Sama's father, were you?" Judge Piper presses. "Hearing your brother paid her hush money had to be hard to hear, too."

I finally go still.

He knows.

"She was lying," I hiss back, more savagely than I mean to. "Martha wasn't supposed to say anything from the NDA she signed. She was lying to you. But my word's not enough, is it? You think I was the one who murdered her, too, don't you?"

He frowns. "No one is saying anything. But I wanted to make it clear your threats have no place here, Orpah. One phone call to the bank, and I'll get all the proof I need regarding your brother; you know Morris wouldn't hesitate to show me who gave Martha the money. So, play nicely. That's all I'm asking here."

"You're hardly asking." I look around, glancing at the crowd, who had largely stopped paying attention to me.

"I shouldn't have to," Judge Piper says again. "I voted for your pies every year I've been on the judging panel. You can win fairly still, even against Martha. But you'll have to do your best."

He starts to walk away, and then he turns around sharply.

"That's it, isn't it?" Judge Piper comes up to me again, his eyes burning into mine. "You used Martha's pies to win the contest, didn't you? That's how she bought your silence about me and Matthias for all these years, and that's why she never entered the contest. She didn't want to risk your wrath."

I swallow hard, suddenly wishing I'd murdered Martha a long time ago, and a lot more violently.

"You don't have any proof," I snap back. "You're just an old man, full of grief at the sudden loss of your would-be sweetheart."

He stares back at me, long and hard, and I have to do my best not to squirm.

"I guess we'll find out when I judge your pie." He shakes his head. "The proof is in the pie filling this time, Orpah. If you win, I'll give up on this—you and your business, and your so-called charity, too. But if you lose, nothing will stop me from destroying everything you've built up with your lies."

"I'll get you disbarred for this," I threaten back.

Judge Piper finally chuckles. "Try it. Getting me disbarred from a pie contest ruling is one for the books, that's for sure."

He excuses himself before I can say anything else. Sherry appears beside me, asking me if I need some water or something to eat since I look so pale.

All I can think of is Judge Piper's threat—and whether or not he actually has any proof against me, and whether or not that proof would hold up in a court of law.

The easiest thing to do to solve this is to just win the contest.

But there was a problem with that.

"I need to make a few personal calls," I say to Sherry. "Excuse me."

I walk a short distance away.

First, I dial my grandmother. I can only hope she's still able to remember how to use a phone, and that she's not too busy with all her projects.

"Hello?"

I let out a small sigh of relief at the sound of her voice. "Memaw? Is that you? You sound so young. How are things at your Freeman's Farmer Market?"

"It's the Fresh Village Farmer's Market," Memaw says. "Now, why don't you dispense with the small chitchat and tell me why you really called, honey?"

I grit my teeth as I tell her a largely edited version of the truth, and that I'm sending Sherry to go pick up the strawberry rhubarb pie from her. Memaw seems skeptical, but she's delighted I'll be showing off her Market on my show—something I'd been meaning to do anyway, ever since "Be the Change" started airing years ago—and I'm pretty sure she won't ask too many questions. It's not like she has good reception off the highway, and even if she'd managed to improve things since I last visited, I can always tell her she'd missed it.

Memaw wasn't the best at remembering things.

After I'm done talking with Memaw, I hang up the phone and dial my brother. When I can't get a hold of him, I tell Sherry it's time to leave.

"So soon?" she asks, looking around. "Don't you want to take some pictures for your magazine?"

"Later," I say. "I've got to go settle a few things at the bank, and I've got to do it now."

My whole life, I'd been beaten down, pushed aside, cast out; mocked, bullied, and looked down on.

I clenched my fist, chipping one of my strawberry-colored nails.

I've already murdered Martha; now I will bury her—and her godforsaken friends, if necessary.

I wasn't going to let anything stop me now—and certainly not a dead woman.

I deserve this.

I am a winner.

I will do whatever it takes.

No one can stop me.

STRAWBERRY PIE

A GARRETT-WRIGHT FAMILY RECIPE

From the kitchens of Virginia Garrett and her great-granddaughter Alice Wright

STRAWBERRY PIE

Ingredients:

1 cup water

1 cup sugar

4 or 5 TBSP strawberry Jell-O

6 TBSP corn starch

1 baked pie shell

1 cup or more strawberries

Directions:

Place fresh strawberries, slice or whole, in a baked pie shell.

Cook water, sugar, and corn starch together on the stove until thick and almost clear.

Remove from heat and stir in Jell-O. Cool and pour over the fresh berries in the pie shell.

VIRGINIA GARRETT, SHARED BY HER GREAT-GRANDDAUGHTER ALICE WRIGHT

"Our family has a pie contest at Christmas every year as a fun little tradition. This year, there were 12 pies entered and this one came in second place, behind everyone's favorite lemon icebox pie.

"This recipe was handed down to me from my great-grandmother, Virginia Garrett, of Washington Valley in Springville, Alabama. This strawberry pie has been a family and community favorite and staple at holidays and church functions for ages. It's super easy to make and turns out vibrantly colored and tasty every time!"

PIE SPY

A GAMBLER BETS IT ALL

Life of Pies, #6

C. S. Johnson

CHAPTER SIX
Garland Morris

If there's one thing I can count on, living in a small town like Fairmont, it's that there's never usually anything too exciting going on.

And I like that, for the most part.

Really, I'm a simple kind of guy; if there's trouble, I'd prefer it to be of my own making.

But I will say, when there is some excitement, it lights up the whole dang town like Christmas lights. Gossip flows like a newly-discovered well, and the people here lap it up like it's full of life-saving power and they just swallowed a salt lick.

Not that I mind. A little excitement here and there keeps thing interesting, and I firmly believe it was a wise man who said predictability was hell.

But predictability is not the same thing as stability, and it's only a fool who doesn't know the difference.

Fortunately for me, I do.

And it's that difference that I feel in my bones as I walk into the bank in the morning. I'm just a little later than usual; it's a quarter past nine instead of my regular five after, but my coworkers are oddly forgiving today.

I look around at my long-time fellow bank teller, Maryanne, and then I gaze at Amanda, one of my newer bank associates. No one says anything to me, but they're all watching me.

That's when Clyde Montgomery, the current president of our banking outpost, walks out of his office and heads to the small coffee station in our lobby.

He's more of a statue then a person most days. Much like me, he's a fixed point in our community, and more than one person around here takes his cues from Clyde.

I do myself, which is why I stop beside him and give him a polite nod. "Sorry I'm late this morning, boss."

He gives me a nod back, as if to say, "Message received," which is the norm for him.

But then he reaches out, pats me on the shoulder, and lets out a loud sigh. The salt-and-pepper mustache of his flutters in an irritated fashion, but his dark eyes are only full of grief.

"We're all running a few moments behind this morning." He shakes his head. "We've all heard the news, and it's a mighty shame about Martha."

I nod glumly as Clyde fills up his coffee cup, loading it up with cream and sugar. As he stirs them in, he gestures down next to the coffee pot. "My Mellie's sent a plum pie for us today. She's going to be entering the pie contest this year again."

"Oh, really?"

I do my best to smile. I'm a little glad that I have an excuse to be sad, since Mellie's pies don't make me happy.

The pie itself looks nice enough—better than the last pie she'd tried to make, which was burned heavily on top, that's for sure. Mellie used the lattice pie crust look, but it was unevenly burned, with it dark at the rounded end and a little limp in the middle; I wonder if her oven is working right.

Clyde's mustache ruffles. "She's pretty proud of her progress. I imagine she wanted to butter you up some for this year's race."

Mellie would know that I'm a judge in the pie contest this year, along with Charles and the mayor. If Charles were talking to me, I would've made a comment about how I hoped she was getting her bad pies out of her system. But since it's her husband standing next to me—who is also my boss—I only nod.

"How thoughtful of her." I eye the pie dish again; this time, I notice no one's dared to take the first slice.

Well, life is supposed to be an adventure …

Resigned to my fate, I pick up a napkin and a small Styrofoam plate, and I load it up as Clyde watches approvingly. The pie is goopy and sludgy at the same time, and it's hard to cut. With each second that passes, I'm growing more and more uneasy about how it's going to taste.

"Thanks, Morris," Clyde says gruffly. "I know you're a good man. And it's a good day for pie, anyways."

I nod again as I choke down the first bite. The plums seem dried out, even for being in a pie, and I wonder if Mellie forgot the sugar entirely or if she'd been baking with Clyde's Diabetes in mind.

"I'm very proud of my wife," Clyde says. "She's always wanted to be Pie Queen. Just like Orpah, you know?"

"Well, who wouldn't want to be Orpah?" I drown the pie flavor out with a hearty gulp of coffee. "With Martha gone now, she'll likely be the winner again this year. It'll give her a new season's worth of her 'Be the Change' show."

"Hmmm." Clyde shrugs noncommittedly as he grabs another sugar pack and I shove another bite of pie into my mouth. "Well, time to get to work, Morris."

I swallow hard as we part ways. He's practically ancient, but he makes a beeline for his office. More than once, he's slipped away for a business call and ended up taking a nap instead.

I'm certain that's why he's lived as long as he has, and when he finally decides to retire and I'm promoted at last, I'll be proud to follow his illustrious example. Making naps a priority would limit stress, and that's a general enough statement I could use it for a political slogan.

I manage a smile at the thought; I'll have to save that one for him later.

Clyde always enjoys a good political discussion. I've seen him go red in the face talking about everything from the old-school days of the Cold War to recent hot-button topics.

Maybe that's why he needs the naps.

Nothing better than political discussions to get the blood pumping, especially when anything that changes only goes to show nothing changes in the end.

Discretely, I slide my plate of Mellie's pie into a trash can tucked away behind my banking station. Once that's gone, I pull out my drawer and start my day.

"Martha was one of our first loyal customers, you know. Morris actually let her have the loan to start her catering business, did you know? Even though she was abandoned with her Down Syndrome girl and her two sons."

At her station beside me, Maryanne is whispering the usual gossip over to Amanda.

"Why would the bank deny her a loan because of her situation?" Amanda asks. I can tell she's younger by the confusion in her voice. Young people today don't understand much about the past. "That seems discriminatory to me."

"Times were different then," Maryanne whispers back, clearly failing to remember her own blatant disgust at the thought of Martha's infidelity. "She shoulda been more focused on her children, not her business, and that was the general way of thinking."

I keep counting my drawer and checking off my notes; I've already heard the news about Martha, but it's always interesting hearing the gossip.

The two women begin to chat some more, but I quickly lose interest in the conversation. I'm lost in the usual rhythms of my job—getting my drawer counted, answering the phone, and checking in on the small drive-through we'd installed a few years ago. All of it is very routine stuff, but I'm happy to do it. It's only when they bring me into the conversation that I give them my attention again.

"Today, Orpah's supposed to announce what flavor her pie's gonna be for the contest," Maryanne says. "What are you betting on, Morris?"

"She won with blueberry last year," I recall, thinking of the warmth and love I'd tasted in the slice. The memory's such a stark departure from the woman herself, and from the plum pie still sticking to my teeth.

"I'll bet she does something with raspberries or strawberries, then," Amanda says. "She seems to go for different things each year."

"I just hope she stays away from chocolate." I put my drawer away as I finish checking my bills and change. "That was Charles' favorite, and he'll be especially bitter after losing his Martha. She'll lose if she does that, and that's a safe bet."

Maryanne huffed. "If he was really sweet on her, it's for the best she's not entering, then. That wouldn't be fair."

As Maryanne and Amanda take turns ranting at each other, I slip back into my own thoughts.

I frown at the thought of my friend. I wonder how Charles is doing with all of this. I heard Matthias was in town, too, and everyone knew what kind of trouble he'd given Martha.

Assuming he didn't kill her himself.

Solomon McCain, our local sheriff, said that he'd heard from Brady, the EMT who was called to the scene, that there was no direct evidence of foul play. But then Solomon said that was something to expect from professional foul play.

Asher, the second son, had called for an autopsy. Matthias had been reluctant. Charles had insisted.

It's all such a sad, sorry, complicated situation.

I'm glad I don't have much to do with it.

The morning goes by quickly, and the afternoon even quicker.

I smile and chat easily with my customers. They always like getting the sense that I'm interested in their lives, and for the most part, I'm happy to give it to them.

Most people are interesting enough, and they're more upfront about it when I treat them as such. A performer's instinct lives inside each of us, and I believe everyone wants to be the kind of person who lives up to others' best expectations.

It's close to closing time before I know it, and my would-be last customer of the day, Aisha Bottoms, the Mayor's wife, is informing me that Orpah hadn't announced her pie officially after all.

Apparently, the news of Martha's death had shaken her.

"Shaken her something fierce," Aisha whispered. "Like the very devil was in the cameraman's lens."

"I can't see Orpah standing for that," I say. "She loves her camera, and all the attention that comes with it."

That's when the little bell at the top of our front door chimes, and all of us look up in surprise as Charles comes through the door.

"Morris." He nods his hello to me, and then waits patiently as I hand Mrs. Bottoms her receipt.

Already I know something is wrong.

Just like Mellie's pie, something is wrong. And suddenly, I don't want to be here.

~

"How are you doing, Charles?" My voice is light and friendly, even though the words are weighed by the years of shared interests, conversations, and of course our bets.

I look at the man I've known for years and barely see him. There are large shadows underneath his chestnut-colored eyes, and his hair seems to have turned silver overnight.

The door behind him rings, and another man walks in. I think it's Asher, Martha's son; he has the same eyes and blonde hair, although his nose makes me think of Joe. His eyes are shadowed as much as Charles', and I almost feel bad for him.

"I wish I could say things were better, Morris," Charles murmurs. "Asher and I are here to talk with you about Martha's account. I'd like to look over the records with Asher."

He nods to the man behind him, who snivels.

"Hello, Asher," I say. "It's been a while, hasn't it?"

"Yes, sir," he replies, trying to give me his best polite smile. No one minds when he fails miserably.

"My condolences on your loss. Martha was a fine woman."

"Thank you."

"Morris, we're here on business." Charles interrupts us lightly, but his voice is as firm as ever.

"What kind of business?"

"We would like a print out of Martha's bank account activity, going back the last twenty years."

It's here I hesitate. There's an urgency in his voice, and I have a feeling I know why.

"I'll need to see Martha's official death certificate before I can allow her beneficiaries access to her account," I say carefully. It's the truth, and we both know it.

But he doesn't like that.

"Morris, you know us. You know we wouldn't be here otherwise," Charles says. "This means a lot to us."

Asher didn't seem so sure about that; likely the judge had strong-armed him into coming here. I look at Asher for help.

"My mother wrote a check for my brother before she died," Asher explains. "He needs to know Mama was good for it."

"Do you have the check?" I ask. "I can cash it for you if you do. That doesn't require a death certificate."

"Morris, there's more important things we need right now." Charles steps up and lowers his voice, pushing Asher out of my line of vision. "We need to see the bank records from fifteen years ago. Martha told me she'd been bought off by Sama's father after Joe left. She said it was her hush money, and she'd signed the NDA. But now that she's dead, we need to protect Sama from the father—and possibly her aunt."

Asher's eyes went wide, and for some reason we both look at each other.

Charles isn't crazy … but grief does make us do crazy things.

"Can you wait until tomorrow? It shouldn't take long to get the needed documents, and you of all people should know that."

It's a coward's play, to ask for time when time is not needed, but as much as I might gamble with money, I hate to think of losing my reputation, especially this late in the game. Clyde was likely going to retire or keel over himself one day soon, and I wanted to be the next president of the bank branch.

"Come on, Morris. This is about more than what's legal; it's about what's right. If you help me now, I'll discharge all your debts against me."

The offer is tempting, especially since I'd prefer to keep my money—and Charles and I go way back, and of course I feel awful about what happened to Martha, and I did know that Asher was her son …

And it isn't like I'd have to worry about Charles spilling the beans about my indiscretion. He was the one asking for it, after all.

Still, I twiddle my thumbs nervously. "Well, you know … "

But before Charles can answer me, the door to the bank bursts open. The chime doesn't even have time to sing out as Orpah Abraham herself comes in. Her phone is clasped between her long, strawberry-printed nails, and I can hear a sharp, Yankee voice over the phone.

" … I can email in the forms just fine," the voice over the phone is saying. "We'll have to check to see that the records met the requirements for sealing, but—"

"But nothing, Kandice! They'll be sealed, or I'll be through with you!" Orpah shouts.

At that moment, I see the crazed look in her eyes as she catches sight of Charles and Asher.

It's then I realize what Charles meant earlier, and just how damning his favor could be.

"You're worried about Orpah, aren't you?" I whisper, and Charles gives me the slightest of nods.

"Clyde Montgomery!" Orpah hollers. "I have business with you!"

From my station, I can hear him snort awake. "What is it?" he grumbles. "Come in."

As Orpah waddles into his office, staring angrily at Charles and Asher on her way in, I bite my lip. "By the look of things, it might be best if you leave now, Charles."

"I need the records," Charles insists. "Asher, tell him."

But Asher only squirms under the judge's sharp gaze. "I think it'll be okay," Asher says. "I've already said I'll come here and live with Sama, and Matthias can find out for himself if the check is good or not. Sama's likely to be considered old enough and competent enough by any judge standard to determine where she'd like to live."

"Asher, I told you, this is important," Charles hisses. "Don't mess this up."

"Why? It shouldn't matter who Sama's father is at this point," Asher continues quietly.

Charles stares daggers as I mull over Asher's defense.

Asher is right; Sama is old enough to handle herself, even with the Down's Syndrome. No one who knew her well in this town would say she was unable to give an account of herself. Charles himself would likely be the one presiding over the case, if it really did come down to it—although I suppose he might recuse himself if he thought he would be too biased.

Matthias might've gotten a check out of Martha, but I already knew she was good for it, more than likely. Martha had struggled with money at times, but she'd never been late on her loan payments for me.

It's only when Charles puts his head in his hands that I understand he's truly hopeless—and he's truly heartbroken.

Whoever gave Martha the money is the one who got her pregnant with Sama.

I look over to Clyde's office, where I can hear Orpah screeching at him about all the years she'd been doing business in here and keeping this old place running.

"Please, Morris," Charles whispers again. "Martha told me the truth about what happened with Sama's father. I only want to get a copy of her bank records to have proof. Asher's here, and you can surely do this small favor for me this one time, can't you?"

"Don't you have a copy of her records from court?" I ask, suddenly wishing I could leave.

"We only needed to fight Joe on the two boys," Charles says, as Asher's face goes pale from the mention of his father. "Martha told me that she'd gotten a check. I need a copy of it, and I'll have all the leverage I need to keep Sama safe from Orpah."

It is at that moment that I recall Orpah had a brother, Omar, who used to work with her. He'd originally wanted to be her program's cook, but she'd abruptly moved him from her show after it was found he'd assaulted several women. Rumors had it that there were worse things he'd done, but no arrests were ever made, and no charges were ever brought up. It helped that Joe Davidson, his best friend and Martha's husband, had always backed Omar's side, declaring him innocent. Orpah moved him to work on the charitable end of her business, and no one in town had heard from him since.

Joe had left shortly after that, too, with little more than a goodbye as he closed his account here. He'd forgotten about it, until he had to come back to face her for their child support hearing.

"Well, all right." I barely hear myself say the words, as I finally pull up the computer screen.

The time on the clock says that it's ten minutes past six, and I know I shouldn't even be on my computer now. It's long past the time to go home—even Maryanne and Amanda had already packed up for the day.

My fingers seem to shake as I type in the required information.

Just as I send it to the printer, the floor rumbles as Orpah exists out of Clyde's office.

"Hold it right there, Garland Morris!"

She's angry.

I put on my most stoic, polite smile. "I'm helping Mr. Piper and Mr. Davidson at the moment, Miss Abraham. I can be with you in a moment."

"Don't give me that," she snaps. "I happen to know you're giving Judge Piper here information about my finances. I want you to stop *this instant*, or you will be fired."

"You can't fire him," Charles interrupts. "We talked earlier about your threats, Orpah, and I'm shocked you didn't think I was serious."

"I am serious, too," she shot back. She holds up her cell phone, which is now silent and blank. "My lawyer and I have filled out the required forms for getting my charity information sealed away. I submitted it to Mr. Montgomery, and he's fast-tracked it for approval. He's a good business man, after all, and he knows my company does a lot of good here in Fairmont. And in this bank, specifically."

Asher surprises me by stepping between them. "I'm only here for my mother's records," he says. "The judge and I wanted to make sure we could find Sama's father."

"Don't tell her that." Charles' voice is nearly inaudible, but Asher swallows hard.

He knows he'd done wrong.

"We weren't here for your financial records," he repeats. Apparently, he hoped this would satisfy Orpah, but he didn't really seem to know her the way the rest of us did.

Orpah begins to chew him out, telling her what a terrible nuisance he is, and that's when Charles catches my eye.

He looks at Orpah, and then at my computer with a long, meaningful glare.

"You know, I'll bet you anything she's got something worth hiding," he whispers pointedly. "Especially given her insistence."

There's a bit of intrigue and compulsion in his voice, and as Orpah starts stamping her foot on the ground, I realize Charles hadn't just come for Martha's records.

He had wanted to get Orpah's too.

He'd been buttering me up for the first request, before he was going to ask me for the second.

"Stop hitting me," Asher yells as Orpah shakes her head and her hair whips into him.

"Stop stalking me!" Orpah shouts back, although she reigns herself in a little more. She pulls out a pack of forms. "You don't have any right to my information, and you won't get it as of tomorrow. Now it's off the clock, and if you try to do anything now, everyone will know it's illegal."

Before anyone else can reply, the door chimes open again, and in walks Officer Solomon McCain.

"What's going on here?" he asks, looking around. "The bank should be closed. As I was driving by, I could hear people shouting."

Clyde steps out of his office. "Yes, we were all just leaving," he says gruffly. "Miss Abraham, you've got your forms. Judge Piper, I'll have to ask you and your acquaintance there to leave as well right now. Morris, you can close up and lock the door behind you."

For a moment, we all remain still, and then Clyde asks, "Would anyone want some of Mellie's plum pie to take home?"

Mellie's pie is on the counter by the coffee, largely untouched after I'd taken my slice.

Officer McCain clears his throat. "I do believe I'll escort everyone out."

Orpah and Asher both leave almost jubilantly, but Charles gave me one last pleading look.

I give him a careful wave as everyone files out of the building.

Outside I can hear Charles talk to Asher and Officer McCain, and I wait until they've all gone home to scoop Mellie's pie into the trash, push it down into the bottom, and head out the back.

Only to pause as I pass by the printer.

I'd forgotten to give Asher and Charles the printout.

Curiously, I skimmed through the long history, recognizing most of it. Martha had her loans, some incoming child support payments, deposits from her catering business, and then, way at the back, she had one large deposit of five hundred thousand dollars, nearly fifteen years ago.

I'd seen it before, but I hadn't looked at it too closely. The only thing that really mattered with those sorts of things is that the check didn't bounce. And it hadn't.

But as I look at the small imprint of the check now, I can just barely make out the name on the signature line.

Omar Abraham.

The address on the check was for "Be the Change Foundation," Orpah's charitable branch for her business.

No wonder she wanted to have her records sealed so badly.

Charles had been right—Martha had been paid off for her silence. She'd never used the money as her own, either, always opting for a loan, like when she'd needed it for her business.

I take the papers and tuck them into my pocket; I'm on my way to resuming my trek to the dumpster out back when I think about that last look Charles had given me.

He'd wanted Orpah's records, too.

Slowly, I look down at the trash bag in my hand. Inside of it, I can smell Mellie's plum pie leftovers.

"I know you're a good man."

Clyde's earlier comment called out to me from what seemed like years ago.

"You know, I'll bet you anything she's got something worth hiding."

Charles' assertion came back to me, too, just as loudly, if not more urgently.

Orpah's records could potentially be sealed as early as tomorrow—although I doubted it. Charity documents were supposed to be open to the public for a variety of reasons.

Still, I put the trash bag down on the floor, and make my way back to my computer.

I clench my fists one last time before typing in a request for the information Charles wanted. I hit the print button, and then shut down the computer like it was diseased.

Once I have the papers, I tuck them into my pocket along with the others, grab the rotting plum pie flavored trash, and get the hell out of there.

All the way home, I just shake my head, muttering to myself. "I don't know about this, I don't know about this … "

I will have to make some calls in the morning; perhaps Maryanne and Amanda will have heard something more by then.

I don't know the specifics of what I've gotten myself into, but I do know one thing for sure—I'm making a big gamble, and until I know the whole truth, I can't say how much it will cost me in the end.

PLUM PIE

A DUNCAN FAMILY RECIPE

From the kitchen of Betty Duncan

PLUM PIE

2 unbaked pie crusts

2 LBS plums

½ TSP lemon juice

½ cup sugar

2 TBSP flour

1 TSP cinnamon

1 TBSP butter

Optional: vanilla ice cream

Preheat oven to 375°

Place one pie crust into a 9" pie dish.

Wash plums. Do not peel.

Cut plums in half, remove pit, and then cut into quarters.

Arrange plums in the pie crust and drizzle lemon juice on top.

Mix together sugar, flour and cinnamon, and sprinkle over plums.

Dot with butter.

Place top crust over plums and flute edges to seal crusts together. Cut slits in top crust.

Bake at 375° for about 65 minutes, checking to make sure it doesn't brown too much. If pie does start to brown too much, place some aluminum foil over the top of the pie and cook until done.

Cool and serve warm or cold. Top with vanilla ice cream if desired.

from

BETTY DUNCAN'S DAUGHTER, PATRICIA DUNCAN CRIDDLE

"My Momma's name is Betty Duncan and she got married when she was 18. She learned to cook after getting married – she was a great cook! If my Daddy asked her to make something and she didn't know how, she would look up in one of the five cookbooks Daddy bought her and make him whatever he wanted. She always said, 'Because I love my husband!'

"When I was a girl, my Momma made these plum pies. My Daddy loved them! I would help cut the plums in half and take out the pits.

"Although I've never made her plum pies myself, I did learn to cook like my Momma. My friends have often told me I should open a little meat-and-three restaurant, but I just enjoy cooking for the church."

SHUT YOUR PIE HOLE

A POLICE OFFICER UPHOLDS HIS DUTY

Life of Pies, #7

C. S. Johnson

CHAPTER SEVEN

Solomon McCain

It's always a rough night after delivering bad news.

As I sit down in my office chair, I can feel the ache in my bones, the kind of pain from troubled slumber. The coffee cup in my hand promises me some escape, and I heartedly take the first sip.

"Ah." I breathe out a sigh of grateful praise. "The first sip is always the best."

There's a giggle at the door, and I look up to see my assistant, Cady Willard, as she peeks in on me. "It's supposed to be good to the last drop."

"That's the brand name stuff," I reply easily. "And we haven't been able to afford that since I was in your position."

Cady grins and holds out a small box of doughnuts. "Perhaps it'll taste better if you have something sweet along with it."

I eye the doughnuts, blithely wishing I didn't have so much self-control. "Well, the Fairmont Spring Festival is still going on, and the pie contest is later. I should save some room for that."

"It's not like you're a pie contest judge," Cady reminds me, putting the box on my desk. "That's just Judge Piper, Garland Morris, and Mayor Bottoms."

"I know. But after they're done, samples are given out to the public. I heard Martha Davidson's last pie is in the running, and I'm curious to see if she's as good as they say she is. Plus, Orpah has another unique creation ready to go this year." I sigh reluctantly. "And you know I can't resist anything she makes."

"Oh, I know how much you love her. I'm sure the rest of the community does, too." Cady nods toward the bookshelf behind me, where, sitting there so gallantly, is a picture of me and Orpah standing together. That was the day she'd endorsed my re-election as Fairmont's sheriff. It had largely been a safe bet I'd win, but her support made me feel more like a winner than actually winning did.

It's also my favorite picture.

I've always admired Orpah. She is a lady of passion, who wants to change the world for the better, and she uses all her power and money and image for good. Sure, she's made some enemies along the way, but then, as a sheriff, so have I.

I didn't always agree with her, especially given her extremely limited experience with law enforcement, but she had admirable ideals. Last year, when Orpah had endorsed me, we'd talked about doing more to rehabilitate criminals, lower bail rates for the Fairmont community, and do our best to believe our enemies could one day be turned to friends.

Who could object to that?

And who would object to the huge check she'd given me from her charity?

Certainly not me. It'd been the first year I'd been given a raise, and if I had to book repeat offenders a few more times, I say I'd earned it.

I give Cady a playful shrug. "Well, all things considered then, I'll pass on the doughnuts for now. I'll get some pie later today when I see Orpah. If I can get her to sneak me an early slice, perhaps I'll see if she'd like an endorsement of mine for Pie Queen."

Cady laughs and takes the doughnuts away, and between her smile and the thought of Orpah's pie, I'm more prepared to face the day.

Or so I thought.

The phone at my desk rings, and I reluctantly pick it up.

"Sheriff McCain," I murmur, picking up my coffee.

"Check the Davidson autopsy for hemlock and ricin."

"Excuse me?" I put my coffee down and lower my voice, suddenly angry at the familiar-sounding voice. "Charles? Is this you? We just talked about this last night."

Once I'd seen them at the bank, I'd decided to take a moment to talk about Martha's death with Charles and Asher. I'd told them both that Brady Simmons, the EMT who'd tended to Martha's body, along with the other two Fairmont medical examiners, agreed there was no evidence of foul play. Asher had been more than relieved at the news, but Charles was quick to say Martha had been murdered—and he suspected Matthias, her delinquent son, as much as he suspected Orpah Abraham.

I'd been shocked at his accusations—a range of them that went back over fifteen years, talking of assault, blackmail, threats, and now murder. It didn't fit Charles' character; he'd always been a very straight shooter, a blunt, quiet type of man who wasn't easily swayed by tears or beauty. When I reminded him of this, and said his stories were pure imagination, he scowled at me like I'd murdered Martha, myself.

Quietly but firmly, I said my goodbyes, and then I'd left them feeling sorry for their loss. I thought I'd been friendly, but now I only feel irritated that my efforts to be friendly and helpful had been in vain.

Should have expected that as a long-time police officer.

Still, I'd expected better of Charles.

I'm about to tell him so, too, when the voice speaks again.

"This isn't Charles. It's not anyone from Martha's family, either." There was a gruff noise, as if the caller had cleared his throat. "I'm calling in a clue. I want to remain anonymous."

I lean forward onto my elbows; the caller isn't in the room, but it's still so easy to get into interrogation mode. "Why should I believe you?"

"You don't have to," the voice replies. This time, there's more fear and impatience in it. "But just check it."

"What if I tell you I need your name, for the official record?"

"The FBI and the IRS let us call in tips anonymously. I don't see why it would matter for this instance."

"Tell me why. Are you the one who gave Ms. Davidson the hemlock and ricin?"

"No. But there was a young man who was just sentenced for killing his neighbor with it. And a very prominent figure with a long-standing grudge against Martha just paid his lawyers."

Ah. So that's the game.

"Let me guess," I say. "Orpah Abraham?"

"Yes. Her 'Be the Change' Foundation has been paying court fees for several cases around the country, but there was an extra check written out this past week for Judge Piper's last case."

"A case the perp didn't win," I remind the caller.

"If he was her drug distributor, wouldn't it be better he went to prison?"

"I think this is reaching," I say. "A lot of this is circumstantial."

"I have the bank records."

Morris. This has got to be Morris.

Garland Morris was Charles' friend, and a loyal one, at that. He'd been at the bank yesterday, too, and he likely knew more details than most of the public. Still, he has no business sticking his nose in places where it doesn't belong.

More calmly now, I take another easy sip of my coffee. "If they're unofficial, they won't be counted as evidence."

"But there *is* a connection. Why wouldn't you—"

"Look, sir, I understand this is a tragic event. I know many people who are directly affected by Ms. Davidson's loss. But the concerted effort to frame Ms. Abraham is ridiculous. She's a political idealist. I understand she has a lot of opponents, but from what I've seen, she's done nothing to suggest she's worthy of any real vitriol."

"Just check the autopsy again, then." He cleared his throat again. "If you're right, then there's nothing to show for it. If you're wrong, Orpah should be questioned."

I'm certain it's Morris on the line with me now. He's loyal, but he's been aiming for Clyde Montgomery's position at the bank for too long to want to risk it needlessly.

Which did make me pause.

If it truly is Morris on the phone, he likely believes he has good cause to be— even if Charles did prod him into doing so.

My curiosity gets the better of me. "Is this you, Morris? I know you're friends with Charles. This doesn't look good for you, or him."

"You don't need to know my name for the tip," the voice retorts.

There's less fear this time, and more anger.

"You want to know why I wish to remain anonymous? It's because it's well-known Orpah's been giving money to Fairmont, too, through her political support of you, and by her foundation. I wouldn't be surprised if she's bought off the pie contest judges or threatened them throughout the years somehow. If you're in her pocket, who's to say who's not?"

"I am not bought by Orpah Abraham," I scoff. "I happened to be the best candidate for the sheriff position. Did anyone in Fairmont really want that eighteen-

year-old who'd just graduated high school to be in a position like mine? You ought to watch yourself, sir, and the accusations you make."

"Why do you think I'm making them anonymously?" The voice is hardened with helplessness now, and despite his insistence, I know I've won.

But I'm a gracious man. A true policeman has to be on occasion, as one must never fail to remember mercy as he is pursuing justice.

"Look, I will do what you ask," I say slowly, "if you tell me your name and where I can come pick you up for official questioning. Otherwise, I have no proof that Orpah is anything other than a smart, tough, lady politician doing her best to serve her community and the people she loves. I highly doubt she's lying or bribing or even threatening anyone else, especially over a pie contest."

There was a long moment of silence on the other line.

"I'll leave a copy of the official evidence at the bank with Morris," the voice finally says. "I'll leave it up to you to decide whether or not you should pick it up."

The line falls silent and goes dead a second later.

Cady knocks at the door. "Hey, Sheriff," she says. "We've got a few requests from the festival people regarding police patrols. Want to run over the numbers? I know it's your absolute favorite thing to do."

Her coy smile and light sarcasm are my salvation, along with the paperwork she's bringing me.

"Sure," I agree. "Give it here. I'll see if I can call around our squad and ask for some volunteers."

Cady blinks in shock, and then hands me the clipboard in her hands. "Well, there's a few other things they asked for, too, just so you know. Word of warning, though: If you work through all of it, you'll likely be late for the Pie Contest."

"I'll take care of it," I say.

My words are flat and emotionless. I know I am avoiding dealing with Morris'
phone call.

The relentless, bureaucratic paperwork from Cady is grueling and boring, and
even more so since I know am doing my job rather than my duty out of a sense of
guilt and procrastination.

However, it's almost blissfully immersing. After more than a decade on the force,
it's easy to almost forget about Morris' call completely.

The sad truth is that even in a small town like Fairmont, even when it's peaceful
and uneventful, the peace never lasts for long. An officer cares for his community,
and that means its future, too—and I have enough trouble preparing for the actual
future; I don't have time to chase after theoretical ones.

It's only when Orpah Abraham herself calls me up and talks to me that I recall
Morris' earlier call.

"Orpah," I crone as she says my name. "I've just finished getting some more
volunteer police to help patrol the festival. You should be safer than Fort Knox."

"Well, I'm relieved to hear that," Orpah replies. "Solomon, I swear, you have
eased my mind like nothing else. I've had a very rough week, as everyone else has, I
know, but I'm afraid I have more reason than ever to believe I'm being stalked."

"Well, you're a famous lady," I remind her. "Surely you know you have a lot of
fans, as well as enemies."

"I know, but this time is different." Her voice turns ominous. "I have names this
time. There's men out there, working to bring me down, just as the Pie Queen
contest is about to be judged."

"I see." I'm certain I know what she's going to say by now, but Orpah is a
woman I admire and trust, and I don't want her to think I've been passive while
she's been pressured. "Would this have anything to do with Martha Davidson?"

"What have you heard?" Her voice is tight.

"Well, I was at the bank last night, too," I remind her. "I know Judge Piper and you were having words with each other. I suspect he's having trouble grieving and he's not able to do much more than blame someone."

"Yes, yes, that's exactly right," she murmurs. "The reason I am calling you directly, Sheriff, is that I want you personally to watch him and Morris during the pie contest. I know they're old friends, and I'm sure Judge Piper, despite his well-known reputation for justice, has been too emotionally compromised by Martha's death. He seems to think I'm to blame for her death, which is just absolutely awful to even say. Martha was a dear friend of mine."

I bite my tongue on that one. Martha and Orpah had never been friendly, so far as I'd known, and I'd be willing to bet they weren't actually friends. But Orpah undoubtedly knew of Martha's influence in the town, and she wouldn't want to put people off with a controversial opinion.

At least, not right now, but perhaps later, after some time had passed and people were able to think more clearly, with the emotional upheaval of her death so recent.

"Her pie is up for judgement, too, apparently, even though that seems like it should be against the rules, and if I win, which, of course, will only happen by the grace of God himself, this will be thirteen years in a row—a historic first."

"And you want to shatter that glass ceiling," I add with a smile.

"Yes."

"I'll be happy to come and supervise," I agree. "I'll head over right now. Are you on your way there, too? I know the pies are due to appear soon."

"Yes, my driver is taking us there shortly," Orpah says. "Thank you so much for helping me with this, Solomon. You're a wise man, and I am grateful for all that you do for me. I will have to see about getting more contributions to your re-election campaign for sheriff."

"Ah, there's no need for that," I reply, but I do still hope she does it.

I'm not going to lie, the police station could use a few upgrades.

"I'm just happy I can rely on you." Orpah gushes out praise for my integrity, and I feel a few knots tighten in my stomach as I recall Morris' tip.

But I quickly shove them away. How could anyone believe Orpah is a bad person? Sure, she's lost a few elections, but she genuinely radiates a deep concern for people, even people like me. And she doesn't give up. She's known for her persistence.

"There are just so many people jealous of me," she says with a sigh, and I quickly nod, even though she's not there. "If I didn't know Judge Piper had a solid record of judgment behind him, I'd ask to have him replaced. I'm sure you're a much better judge of pie than he is. What do you think about seeing if Mayor Bottoms will replace him? And Morris, too?"

"Well, I doubt that will happen," I say, suddenly uneasy. "Besides, you don't want the community to say that you asked them to change judges fearing you'd lose. Judge Piper is a good man. Grieving, perhaps, but still good. And Morris knows his place in the community. He wouldn't risk that. Not needlessly."

It's the second time I've thought so, and the more I think of it, the more I know it's true.

And I hate to think of what that means.

"Well, if you trust they'll be able to vote with integrity, I'll believe you," Orpah says. "After all, you're a man of high integrity yourself."

There's a small hint of disappointment in her voice, but I'm not sure what she expects from me.

"Yes, ma'am," I say readily, although I'm a little irked now.

This whole morning my integrity has been tested. First by Morris, and then by Orpah.

I don't know what is worse, either: Morris believing my integrity is bought off by Orpah, or Orpah believing that I have enough integrity that I could safely bend the rules for her.

Either way, I decide it's time to hit the road, and head over to the festival.

~

As I drive past the festival welcome center, I slow down my police car and look around with a sense of pride. The Fairmont Festival Board is led by some of the best community organizers Fairmont's ever had, and despite Fairmont's dwindling population, we seem to get more visitors here each year.

The Fairmont Spring Festival is a smaller, more intimate festival than what's seen in movies, but I like to think it's just as sweet and nostalgic. Our festival has a dunking booth, a Hole-In-One golf game, several carnival trucks with treats, and even a rock wall now, to appeal to the young'uns. The town's gotten some good sponsors, too, over the years, thanks to Orpah's participation in the Pie Queen Contests. There was a tent that housed the National Guard, some political tents for more local elections and smaller, more unusual political PACs. Several of the churches have stations, too, where they all try to out-evangelize each other while also trying to avoid all the tattooed New Agers.

By design, the Pie Queen Contest is set up in the back of the festival, and because I'm a well-known VIP—a policeman, and the sheriff at that—I get to take the back road that goes all the way 'round, and then I'll get to walk right up to the Pie Contest. There aren't too many people with that privilege.

So, I'm a little surprised to see another car shuffling along the pathway in front of me.

The small, bland, red Camry seems to have some radiator troubles, but the tag is from out of state. I keep this in mind as I pull over, get out of my car, and practice my "Can I help you get out of this restricted area?" speech in my head.

It's a pretty standard speech.

The car finally rocks to a stop and slides off to the side of the road.

A woman with a wild and styled afro steps out. She is wearing a badge, indicating her role as one of Orpah's entourage. I think I recognize her as I see her pull out a small, pie-sized box.

It's a small, pretty package, with a fancy design all over. Spurred on by the hope of getting a sneak peek at Orpah's pie, I hurry forward and smile.

I'm about to call out a hello when she reaches into the car and pulls out a glass pie pan.

I stop and watch as she tugs off the wrapper and moves the pie from its foil pan to the glass one.

What is going on?

I can't help but remember the pie from last year as I stand here. It was in a ceramic pie pan, with pretty violet and rose flowers. It was a blueberry pie, perfectly made with love and the sweetest whipped cream on top, made with a bowl-like crust.

Orpah made it very clear she loved her blueberries.

I slide over, still watching Orpah's employee as she tries to discreetly dispose of the package in her car.

The only thing that makes me hesitate is how distressed she seems.

"I can't believe this," she mutters with a sigh, just loudly enough for me to make out her words.

She turns on her heel and carries the pie toward the Pie Queen display, where other pies are already waiting to be judged. I can see Orpah there, herself, laughing and smiling in her trademark bright colors, her ruby lips and alabaster teeth brightening up the entire display.

Ruefully, I follow slowly after her employee with the fake pie.

I can only hope that it's Orpah's own specialized packaging, and that maybe I'm over-anxious because of Morris' call. I know I'm just feeling a tad bit guilty that I haven't followed up on his hinting, and that's why I'm worried.

I pass by the Camry, and I can see the packaging label on the front seat. My heart sinks.

In big, bold letters, the words "Memaw's Homemade Pie" loop under smaller words that spell out "Fresh Village Farmer's Market."

I look back at the Pie Queen display, just in time to see Orpah heading over to her employee with the fake pie.

Immediately, I duck down behind the Camry. Inching closer, I move along the ground—and wince at the pain that comes from using stealth tactics—as I listen to their conversation.

"—about time you got here, Sherry," Orpah snaps, shocking me with how loudly her voice lashed out. "I've been waiting for nearly an hour."

"The traffic getting back here from the Interstate was hard to deal with," says the employee, whose name I deduce is Sherry. "I still don't see why you needed me to buy this. I thought you said you didn't like Martha that much. Why are you so upset at her death that you can't bake?"

"Hush your mouth, or I'll make sure you never work in public relations ever again," Orpah hisses. "Do you know how easy your reputation in this field can be destroyed? No? Well, I'll show you, if you keep this up. This was your idea, remember?"

My mouth drops open in shock, and my breathing goes shallow.

No! No, don't say anything else, Orpah!

I want to scream at her, but nothing comes out of me; I'm too stunned—and as much as I hate to admit it, scared.

"No, please don't do that," Sherry begs Orpah.

"You were the one who insisted we make history today." I can almost hear Orpah jabbing her long, painted fingernail into Sherry's chest. "I was toying with the idea of backing out gracefully, but *no*. We had to make history!"

"You wanted to make history," Sherry says, her voice breaking. "And I'm understanding and sympathetic, I swear. But I thought you made your own pies."

"*I do*," Orpah insists. "And I'll sue anyone who says otherwise. Remember, we have an NDA between us for your time working with me, don't forget. So, if you want to keep your money and your employment, you'll straighten up, smile, and convince everyone you see that I'm a goddamned joy to work for."

I am paralyzed with incredulity as I stand there and listen to her ranting, but all I want to do is scream at her myself.

"What are you saying? What are you doing? Shut your pie hole, because people could be listening!"

That's what I want to yell, because I desperately want Orpah to *not* be this way.

Orpah had always championed women's advancement in their chosen career fields. Why would she threaten to ruin this young lady's future?

And all over a pie!

But I already knew the answer. It's as plain as day.

"You were my hero," Sherry murmurs, her voice full of sadness.

I shake my head down in shame; I could've said the same thing myself.

"Please, don't give me that. You know who needs heroes? Losers who aren't capable of handling their own problems. Now, let's go. People are waiting for me."

I wait until I'm sure they're gone before I stand up.

From where I'm standing, I can see others starting to arrive. I see Edith Hennessey and Clarice Youngblood, Martha's closest friends. I'd heard the rumors that Martha had given them a pie before she'd died and that they were entering it into the competition on her behalf. As I watch, I notice Clarice is carrying a pie herself, while Edith has hold of Donnie, her ill-tempered husband.

I see Judge Piper coming toward the table. Each year, he looks forward to Pie Queen Day with aplomb, but this year it looks as though Martha's death has made some part of him die, too.

Orpah is worried that he'll pick Martha's pie over hers as a matter of bias, but I can't stop myself from thinking she doesn't deserve to win anyway.

Not after what I'd just witnessed—not after what I'm witnessing now.

As Mayor Bottoms arrives and the crowd starts to gather, Orpah dazzles the crowds with her old stories, the old calls for running for office; I can hear her assurances that she's able to do more for women and poor folks and minorities and such without being in office, but the more she talks, the more miserable Sherry looks, and the more the knots in my stomach continue to tighten.

As Mellie Montgomery approaches the Pie Queen station, followed by some of the other women of Fairmont, I start to slink back to my cop car.

They're only waiting for Morris to show up.

And I know where he is.

He's waiting for me.

As I buckle in, I radio Cady and let her know to send for another policeman. I need someone to monitor the area while I make a quick detour.

"Alright, boss, should be easy enough to do that," Cady replies. "Orpah Abraham's called a few times, asking for you. If she calls back, what should I tell her?"

"Tell her I'm on my way. I just got a hot tip from someone on a possible crime and I need to check it out. For my integrity's sake."

"Ooh, she'll like that," Cady says happily. "Do you need anything else from me?"

"Not right now, Miss Cady. Just keep the lights burning for me at the office. It might be a long night after we're done with the Pie Queen Contest here."

~

I walk into the bank just a few minutes after four. It's expected to close early tonight, for the festival's sake, but Clyde is nowhere in sight, and only Amanda and Morris appear to left watching over the building.

Clyde would want to cheer on his wife, I recall, thinking of Mellie's terrible baking skills.

I catch Morris' eye, and he quickly looks away.

He already seems guilty.

But then, I am, too.

On the way over to the bank, I'd replayed the conversation between Orpah and Sherry over and over in my mind.

Orpah had seemed to glitter, so brightly and profusely, like a star that had fallen to Earth on a dark night, promising to abolish all the darkness in our lives. Somehow, she'd sweet-talked her way into my trust, and I'd given it to her without so much as a second thought, like a wide-eyed, love-struck sucker.

Shame burns through me as I stand in front of Morris.

I'm tempted to tell him that Orpah is cheating to get her title of Pie Queen, but I can't bring myself to say anything about it.

Morris seems to understand my silent query; he merely points to a small pile of papers off to the side of his desk.

"Someone wanted you to have those," he finally mutters, as I take hold of them.

I falter this time, as I look through the first couple of lines.

Morris had insisted earlier that Orpah had paid the lawyers responsible for a recently sentenced perpetrator. He hadn't been wrong.

Unlike Orpah's pie, this wasn't fake.

"Someone wanted me to check the autopsy for hemlock and ricin, too," I reply softly.

"Did you?" He looks away from me.

"Not yet." I shrug and look away, too. "I had a lot of paperwork to take care of earlier. But I'll call Brady and see what he says."

"And you'll update Judge Piper on what he finds tomorrow?"

I shrug again. "We'll see what tomorrow brings. Will you be heading over to the festival soon?"

He nods.

"Well, see you then." I tighten my hold on the papers, and then I turn around and walk out.

Judge Piper had seemed like only part of his real self earlier, and as I walk back to my car, I feel every inch the same.

Sitting down in my car, I turn the key, and head back to the police station.

Cady seems surprised to see me, but I tell her to ask for Brady to report in on any updates for the Davidson case, and then I head over to my desk.

Above my chair on the bookshelf is the picture of me with Orpah.

Her smile is so wide and bright; her enthusiasm is invigorating and joyful, everything anyone would want in a leader.

But now I look at it and see her brown eyes, outlined with liner and accentuated with bright shadows; they seem hollow and dark, empty and fake.

Fake.

It's all fake, isn't it?

I think over my past experiences with Orpah carefully, weighing each moment diligently. After I recall her yelling at her employee, I only shake my head.

No, not all of it was fake.

But it still stings, that I was taken in by an illusion—an illusion I wanted to be real, and one I still wanted to be real enough to keep me from having to do what I must.

Quietly, I lay the picture facedown.

"There's going to be hell to pay for this," I murmur.

And then I sit down and begin to fill out the reports, drawing up the paperwork for a formal investigation. Brady calls me as I put the final touches on the form.

When I hang up a moment later, it's then that I realize there's no longer any joy at the thought of doing my job—but there's no longer any sharp, twisting pain in my gut, either.

I look down at the forms one last time before I put my pen on the paper and ruefully sign my name.

I'm not doing my job.

I'm doing my duty.

BLUEBERRY DELIGHT

A SIBLEY-ELLIS FAMILY RECIPE

From the kitchens of Sarah Francis Sibley Ellis and her daughter Letitia Ellis Taylor

BLUEBERRY DELIGHT

Ingredients:

CRUST

1 cup chopped pecans

½ TSP salt

¾ cup plain flour

1 stick butter

FILLING

2 cups sugar

2 packages Dream Whip

2 8-oz packages cream cheese

1 can blueberry pie filling

Melt butter and mix in flour, salt, and pecans. Press into a Pyrex dish and bake at 275° for 25-30 minutes. Let cool completely.

Mix Dream Whip as directed, then add sugar and softened cream cheese. After crust is thoroughly cooled, pour filling over it.

Spoon one can of blueberry pie filling over the entire top of the pie. Swirl the pie filling on top with a fork to give it a marbled look. Refrigerated until firm and serve.

from
CRYSTAL MCGOUGH, SARAH FRANCIS SIBLEY ELLIS, AND LETITIA ELLIS TAYLOR

"Another recipe passed down from my pecan-farming grandparents, there's no wonder even my grandmother's blueberry pie has a pecan crust. I remember, when I was a child, my mother using this recipe, not with canned blueberries, but with fresh blackberries my brother and I would pick from a blackberry bush that grew on the fence in our backyard. It was a favorite springtime tradition, picking fresh berries and enjoying this family recipe.

"The house next door, which shared that particular fence with us, would change owners every 2-3 years. One of our most short-term neighbors, soon after moving in, set fire to our blackberry bush and the bush never grew back. Those neighbors moved shortly after that. Talk about a core memory!

"While the bush is now gone, the recipe lives on, passed to a new generation. Whether made with blackberries or blueberries, this pie is sure to be one the family will love.

APPLEY EVER AFTER

A BROKEN HEART SEEKS TO HEAL

Life of Pies, Book 8

C. S. Johnson

CHAPTER EIGHT
Pamela Pearson

I grit my teeth together in muted fury as I stare at my computer screen. It's slowly loading my email, but the wi-fi is spotty here in Asher's hometown of Backwardsville, USA, and I need to check on my grades and get some work done.

Seconds pass before the loading screen times out, and a pop-up lets me know there's "connectivity issues."

I just want to scream, pull at my hair, and wave my fists at the ceiling in rage.

But I know I can't.

I don't want someone to see me acting like a loon; even though I'm practically barricaded inside Asher's old room at the far end of the hall, I don't want to take any chances and further ruin Asher's opinion of me.

My shoulders slump forward; I've already done a huge amount of irreparable damage.

I just want to cry; I feel so hopeless.

Instead, I slam my laptop cover down, as angrily and gently as possible. My mother always commended me on my enormous amount of self-control—something she knew absolutely nothing about.

I swat the thought away from me as if it were a passing fly.

I don't want to think about *my* family, least of all while I'm hiding from Asher's.

"Of course there are connectivity issues," I mutter under my breath as I stand up, desperate to find another distraction.

It isn't hard.

Once more, it hits me that I'm in Asher's old room, where he lived and slept and worked for several years as he earned enough money to go to college. I can feel my anger lessen as I look around his room.

There are so many things I admire about Asher, really.

He grew up even more poor than I did, and he's still a much better person than I am.

Not only does he work hard, love on his mama, and care for his sister, but he's never bothered by the thought of working hard and putting in effort to get done what needs done.

He's still slow about some things—I had to nag him endlessly to get him to move in with me, even though it was clear we were both smitten, and I needed help with the rent—but he's authentic and truly loving. And he doesn't have to be duplicitous about his motives.

Pure, unrelenting guilt slices through my heart all over again as I catch sight of the clock.

It's just after five, and the pie contest at the Fairmont Spring Festival is going to get started soon. Asher went out with Judge Piper, his mother's boyfriend, hours ago, trying to get an autopsy and forensic reports and who knows what else. The judge seemed to be going through a classic case of denial, and once more, Asher is dragging his feet, following someone else's lead, unable to say no or properly stand up for himself.

Assuming he wants to at all.

Judge Piper has it in his head that Orpah Abraham, the local goddess of TV talk shows and philanthropist extraordinaire, is behind the death of Asher's mom—or maybe he's just using that as a pretext to get Matthias thrown in jail. Personally, after all I've seen and heard, it's not the most implausible idea.

It truly doesn't help that Matthias is an absolute tool.

From the few sentences he's grunted at me, I'm hardly thrilled he's come home for Asher's visit.

Asher and I had talked about our families before, somewhat, but I was more than happy to change the subject. I don't like thinking of my parents back in Ohio. My mom had married my dad when he'd gotten her pregnant, and for the most part, they agreed it was best to stay together. But it was far from marital bliss. I was only seven when I first caught my father cheating, and my mom seemed to take this as a challenge; in the following years, she would take "night classes" and go on "work conferences," both frequently and randomly. I knew by the time I was in middle school they were "white trash," and now that I'm in graduate school, only months away from securing myself in my profession, I don't want to deal with them at all.

I don't want to lie to Asher, but some days, it is tempting to tell him that they died.

I glance down to see some of Asher's photographs on his desk. He's got his Mama and Sama, and Matthias, and there's even an old picture of his dad that's tucked away behind some of the other frames.

I pick up the picture of Asher in his high school graduation cap. It's only from a few years ago, and at the sight, I can't help but miss him.

Everything in this room is him: the sunny windows, the worn-in carpet that's been carefully cleaned, the warm flannel of his bedspread; there is a large deer crossing sign hung up, hopefully as a joke, and a bookcase full of books about everything from cooking to finance to hunting and fishing to comics, and even his old Bible, with his name in simple gold-lettered engraving … everything here makes me think of a simple redneck, but one who is so optimistic and wholesome, with a quick smile and a solid heart.

I want him back. I want "us" back.

I miss our mutual work-at-home nights, where he would cook up something quick and nice, and we would curl up together on our couch while he worked on classwork and I would get my internship material organized. We would half-watch a movie or a sports game. Asher doesn't like movies much, and I don't know anything about sports, so we'd compromise and switch off. It didn't matter that much whatever we watched, since we just had a good time together.

We were just so happy. Dedicated to our jobs and each other. That was all I wanted.

I close my eyes and take several deep breaths, counting slowly to ten, hoping I will gain some clarity and lose some stress.

But as I finish, I know my breathing exercises haven't done me any *real* good.

I pull out my phone, wondering if I should just give up and call Asher myself. I'm just about to give in when it happens.

Bang!

A loud noise sounds out from the room next to Asher's, and I flinch as another *bang* echoes through the old walls of the house.

I inch toward the door, hesitating. I'd closed the door tightly when I came in after lunch, pretending I wanted to "take a nap" since I "had trouble sleeping." I don't really know why I bothered to lie; no one seems to even really care what I do.

A new small series of *crash-bang-boom* rings out, and I hear Matthias call out from the living room.

"Damn, Sama, stop it before you get hurt!"

Suddenly, I know what is happening: Sama, Asher's beloved little sister, is throwing a fit in her room.

I ignore the softer banging noises as I try to picture what she is doing. From the sound of it, she's throwing something against her wall, or maybe she's belly-flopping all over the floor.

I don't know what her usual bad temper moments look like. Ever since Asher and I arrived, she has been moping around the house, and I can't blame her; grief is hard enough on normal people, and losing a mother she loved has to feel even more awful. And then on top of that, it has to be difficult for her to properly express her sadness.

I know this is my chosen field of work, but I've wisely decided not to interfere. In my counseling classes, I've been taught how to approach disabled people, but I have never had a raw, unmonitored, up-close encounter with one before.

So … it's not my fault that I don't really know what to do.

Right?

I shake my head. Quietly, I put my phone into my pocket with a sense of shame.

It's terrifying to think my degree hasn't prepared me for this kind of situation. I'm five years in, and I graduate soon, and I'm not prepared for *this*.

Of course, I haven't been prepared all week. Asher's mom dying *was* a pretty big shock, too. Hearing she was murdered was another big surprise—if she was murdered at all.

I certainly don't know.

I let out a quiet sigh. "But then, who can really know crazy?"

My hands cover my mouth instinctively, and I try to smother my shock at hearing my own inappropriate thoughts.

Really, that's something I *shouldn't* say—and I know it.

What was the point of becoming a counselor if I don't think it's possible to truly reach those kinds of people?

Carefully, I peel my hands away from my mouth, determined to remain silent. I bite down on the inside of my cheek, desperate for some redirection.

I eye my computer again, but I hesitate as I reach for it.

Asher and I had agreed originally we would absolutely not worry about work or school while we were visiting with his mom, and I'd mostly meant to honor that promise.

But now we're here and his mom is dead, his family is in chaos, and Asher isn't speaking to me.

Work is the best option I have for avoiding everyone else.

But there's another *bang* from Sama's room, and Matthias is already yelling again.

"Sama, stop it," Matthias hollers. "You're just making it worse."

Frankly, I want her to stop, too, but it's at the harsh annoyance in his voice that I clench my fists.

Carefully, carefully, almost with a resigned, painful acceptance, I stand up straight, smooth out the wrinkles in my shirt, make sure my hair has been tamed, and make my way to the door.

Yes, I don't know what to do with Sama.

But I've already done a terrible job at helping Asher through this agonizing time, and if I am really in love with him, I ought to do my best to fix things.

Right?

Suddenly, I stop in my tracks. My own past traumatic scars scream at me, telling me not to interfere—that stepping up to help would just be another useless exercise

in selfless serving, that I would get burned by Asher in the end anyway, and even Asher himself wasn't home to help, so why would I even bother?

Why *should* I even bother?

Aren't my parents a prime example of this? That there's no point in giving someone a part of you that you can't take back, and that there's nothing that lasts forever, and that even with the best of intentions, it's better to control your relationship than let it be an actual partnership?

I sigh and put my head in my hands.

When I was growing up, I knew my parents didn't have a "happy" marriage. As I got older, I soured toward the idea of marriage entirely; I didn't want to be like my father, running around with a new lover every other month, while still giving the money to the spouse; and I didn't want to be like my mom—worried about STDs and paying for secret abortions after having sex with strange men. Why both my parents stayed married to each other, I couldn't imagine; my best guess was that it would make them publicly look bad, and they never had enough money to make divorce look publicly good.

I figured I could be a different person from both of my parents. I could learn from their mistakes. I would make better choices.

And then I grew up, and life hit me hard.

I had several boyfriends, both serious and non-serious, but slowly, as the relationships ended and the hope began to fade, I began to realize how little I enjoyed spending time with them. I hated giving myself away, only to have the men wind up as losers, liars, and louses. And none of them gave me anything that was worth keeping at the end of it all.

Even when I focused on finding a rich man to take care of me, I soon lost interest. Money can make a man interesting, but if it's the only thing, it's not enough to keep me interested.

I'd given up on men and dating altogether when I'd met Asher.

Sure, he was behind in his schooling, and he wasn't likely going to get rich, but he was the first man in a long time that seemed to really like me, and really wanted something from me that would last longer than a few months. Slowly, maybe even so slowly I didn't notice it, he'd made me hope again.

He was just different. And he cared about me, genuinely, not because he was getting sex or because we were living together or anything distinctively transactional.

That was the entire reason I agreed to come out here with him, even if I'm currently having a lot of second thoughts and plenty of doubt.

Bang!

"Damn it to hell, Sama, that's enough!" Matthias yells.

I hear him get up; his feet stomp loudly across the room and down the hall, and I'm scared he will hurt Sama.

My resolution strengthens, and I open my door just in time to see him reach Sama's room.

"What's wrong?" I ask, keeping my tone as mild and firm as possible.

"Sama's throwing herself down onto the floor from her desk," Matthias snaps. "I'm surprised you didn't hear her already. She's going to bring down the house next, and all for some attention."

"It's natural to want some attention," I murmur, scooting in front of him and stepping into Sama's room. "Um … "

The room before me looks like a bit of a warzone. There are art supplies, including paint and glitter, all sitting around in piles on the floor and various surfaces. Her bed isn't made. A small, old rocking chair with a well-worn cushion stands by the closet, which is bursting full of clothes and toys. Some storybooks, books more appropriate for children, are on the bed.

Sama is on the floor, too, rolling around as she silently cries. Asher hadn't told me much about his sister, other than he loved her and he'd mentioned a few of her favorite things here and there, but I hadn't realized how old she was. She was like a large toddler, and she looked up at me with her wide-set eyes in angry suspicion.

Almost like she knows I don't really want to be here—almost like she knows I don't really know what to do.

"Hi, Sama," I say softly, feeling awkward already. My voice is more high-pitched than usual, like I'm trying to hypnotize her or something. It makes me feel like a fraud, but I hold my ground. "I'm Pamela. Do you remember me?"

She ignores me and turns over on her side, facing away from me.

Matthias groans. "Just leave her alone. If she's not singing and dancing, she's having a tantrum or giving someone the silent treatment. Just like a regular woman, if you ask me."

Sama lets out a small moan, and I clench my fists again, tempted to slap Matthias—both for his rudeness, and for making me feel like he's calling me out on my behavior for the past couple days.

"Why don't you call Asher and see where he's at?" I suggest, hoping to get rid of Matthias. "I'll help Sama clean up her room."

Matthias lets out a dismissive huff. "Why don't *you* call Asher? You're the one he's going to marry, aren't you? I know he's got Mama's ring."

He glances down at my hand, and then notices I'm not wearing a ring.

He actually seems shocked. He grumbles something that sounds like "never mind, I'll call him," and the sting of his comment is almost worth it just so he'll leave me and Sama alone—*almost*.

I wait until he's gone before I turn back to Sama.

We're alone now, and she is my problem.

"Why don't I help you clean up some?" I offer, glancing around uneasily, but I decide to start with her desk. I pick up some papers and start organizing them into two different piles of "drawn on" and "blank." There are some nice scribbles, and even a nice picture that looks something like her mom.

"This is nice," I say, putting it on top. "You seem to like drawing."

There is no answer, but I can feel her rolling over, back onto her other side. There's no doubt she's watching me as I put her pencils and other crayons, stencils, and erasers into a pencil box and do my best to shut it.

I try to chit-chat with her while I work. She doesn't move a lot, or say anything.

I feel asinine, but I'm grateful for this. I've only heard her talk a little to Asher, and her words sound muffled at times; I don't want to cause her stress by asking her to repeat them.

I pick up her clothes, noticing some faded stains on them. "You should get some new clothes soon," I say, folding them.

"Why?"

Sama's question bothers me, and I blush, remembering that Asher's mom wasn't rich by any means.

Of course, she was still able to give Matthias some money.

"I just thought you'd like some new clothes," I tell her. I bite my lip. "Maybe Asher and I can take you and get a new dress."

I don't say it, but she'll need it for the funeral. That is, assuming we ever have one; Judge Piper was adamant about getting an autopsy and suspecting foul play. I wouldn't be surprised if he had a warrant out on Matthias, or even Orpah, before long.

Recalling Matthias' expression when he realized he'd upset me, I don't think he's the one who did it. If he had, I don't think he'd be so upset at my discomfort. And he seems smart enough to take the cash and run out of town if he did do it.

Sama says nothing as I finish tidying up her room. It's only when I have nothing else to do that she rolls over, stands up, and throws everything off her desk again.

I grit my teeth, but I work on making it clean again.

Look at the bright side; it gives you something to do.

I've just put the last stack of papers back on her desk when she reaches out toward me; Down Syndrome or not, I know she wants to knock everything off her desk again.

"Hey," I say, carefully grabbing her hand quickly. "Let's not do that again, okay? I just cleaned."

"Let go, Pamela!" she snaps, pulling free from me. She makes some noises with her mouth, and I don't know what to do with that.

Before I can stop her, she slides everything off her desk again.

"Let's do something else," I suggest. Redirection was good for Matthias, so maybe it would be good for Sama, too. I try to think of something easy, something she'll like, and then I remember the apples Asher had gotten for her from that old granny lady. "Asher got you some apples the other day. Why don't you help me wash them?"

"And then we bake them?" Sama asks. Her brown eyes have deep shadows underneath, but I can see a sudden spark of interest in her gaze.

"Okay." I steel myself as I nod. I feel like my body needs to take over and tell my mind what we're doing, since I really don't want to actually do it. "We can bake them."

Sama is instantly cheered up by this, and she takes my hand and leads me to the kitchen.

The kitchen where her mom died only a few days before.

After she'd just cooked a meal for Matthias.

I try really, really hard not to think of this as I gather up the apples and start looking around for dish towels and other things I think we'll need.

"Here." Sama hands me an ugly apron. It's frilly and lacy, and the flannel pattern on it makes me feel like a matronly scarecrow.

"Mama likes this one," she says, and I feel even worse as I reluctantly tie it on.

At least it will protect my clothes from the cooking stuff.

It turns out I don't have to worry about that too much; Sama seems to know what she's doing. I watch as she pulls out the flour and salt and apples, and even some vanilla and sugar and cinnamon.

"Did you bake with your mother a lot?" I ask tentatively, as I wash the apples and she cuts them.

"Yes," Sama said. "I like to bake. Mama and I do it a lot. I help her with her business."

"Oh, her catering business?" I vaguely recall Asher mentioning his mother's company as I watch Sama nervously. She handles the paring knife in her hand well enough, despite her youth and disability. I'm relieved and impressed that she doesn't cut herself.

Frankly, even with my age and relative cognitive functions, I'm not sure I'd be able to do the same.

"Mama is the best baker in the world," Sama says. "Everyone in town says so. Except for Orpah Abraham. I don't think she likes Mama. When she comes to visit, they yell a lot and I hide."

"I see," I reply. "Does she come often?"

"She came this week. She was really mad when Mama told her she wouldn't be making her pie this year."

"Her pie?" I wipe down the counters again—heart attack or not, I don't want any germs around from Martha's death as I bake a pie with Sama. "I heard the next-door neighbor lady say that Martha—I mean, your mom—had a pie at her house and she would be entering."

"Not Mama's pie," Sama explains. She pulls out some flour and begins mixing it with all kinds of other things—yeast, I think, and some sugar and salt. "Orpah's pie. She's the Pie Queen because Mama makes her pies every year."

"What?" I stop cleaning, but I'm still not focused enough for me to process what Sama just said. "What?"

"Mama makes Orpah's pies." This time, Sama whispers the words, as if she's remembering she's not supposed to say anything. "That's how Mama keeps her away from me and Pip."

"Oh." My mouth feels like its clogged, and I try to remember what my counseling classes have said about client privilege and when I need to worry about reporting things to the police.

If I need to report this at all.

I mean, Orpah Abraham being crowned Pie Queen for the Spring Festival for twelve years in a row because of another woman's pies wasn't against the law—just the contest rules.

"She was pretty mad," Sama continues as she pulls out some wax paper and a roller. "She yelled at Mama when she came to see her."

"I can imagine a big celebrity like Orpah wouldn't want a big secret like that out in the open," I agree tepidly.

I'm really not sure what to do.

Part of me really secretly relishes the gossip; this is the kind of career-destroying lie that the tabloids dream about. The other part of me says Sama could be lying, or just telling stories, and I'm just leaning into that theory when Sama comes over to me and gives me quick hug.

"Thanks, Pama," she says. "I like baking with you."

I'm left completely speechless. First by the sincerity behind her words, and then because she'd called me "Pama."

It sounds weird to me, but it also makes me feel as though she accepts me as part of the family.

Sort of.

In a very lighthearted, very superficial kind of way.

Sama's mom has just died, she has Down Syndrome, and she's definitely very sad and everything has departed drastically from its usual routine. As limited as I am in my counseling experience with disabled people, I know I don't have a right to her affection.

But she's given it.

And that makes me feel worse.

"Oh, well, you're welcome," I finally murmur. "I don't think I'm much help. Asher is the one who likes to cook."

"Bake."

"Yes, bake." I'm just about to tell her how Asher and I met when Sama grabs a cookie cutter and starts to cut the pie crust she'd rolled out. "Um, what are you doing? Doesn't that go in the pie pan?"

"Not making pie," Sama tells me as she cuts up the dough into a familiar shape.

"Tarts."

I hear myself say the word more than I realize I say it, as I'm pulled back into that moment where Asher offered me a tart at that seminar class.

"Looks good," Sama says, as she lays out her tarts on a baking sheet. After she makes a few more, she looks at me expectantly. "Help, please."

"Oh … okay." I almost wince as I grab the pie crust and the apples. "I'll try."

I soon forget my insecurities as Sama and I work and make small talk. When we're all done, Sama organizes the baking sheet a little more carefully while I pull out a small bowl and prepare the vanilla and powdered sugar.

As terrible a baker as I am, even I know how to make the icing for tarts.

Maybe if Sama and I can get along, and if the apple tarts turn out decently, maybe, maybe, Asher will forgive me for saying Down Syndrome babies are defective.

Glancing around, I bite back a sigh. I'll need more than a baking sheet full of apple tarts to convince Asher I am sorry about that.

It doesn't help me feel better as I watch Sama work. I wonder about my own half-siblings—if they had lived, if we had gotten along, and if maybe my mother would have been wrong to …

"Pama!"

Sama yelps, and I nearly jump. "What? What is it?" I ask, frantic, wondering if I've done something wrong or if she's been hurt.

"Don't use that bowl." Sama points to the bowl. "*Poison.*"

"Poison?" I repeat carefully.

"I saw her do it," Sama whispers. "She did it to Mama."

"Um …" I don't know what to do with her. Glancing around, I catch sight of Matthias, and I wave him into the kitchen. "Hey, can you come here and help me for a moment?"

I fully expect him to rebuff me, so I'm surprised as he appears in the doorway. "What?" he barks.

"Sama just told me that there's poison in that bowl," I tell him, as she picks it up with a paper towel. She drops it onto the floor, and Matthias steps forward to take it from her.

"Stop that," he says to her. "Do you wanna get poisoned too?"

Sama bursts into tears before she runs howling into her room. I can only hope I won't hear any more banging coming from her room as I glare at Matthias.

"Would you please ease up?" I ask Matthias. "She was telling me that your mom was poisoned."

"Who's going to believe her, even if it's true?" Matthias hisses. "She's retarded, and she's not a credible witness."

"She said Orpah Abraham was here the other day and poisoned your mother," I object. "Didn't you say you saw Orpah Abraham here, too?"

Matthias grunts. "So what? Even if Orpah did kill her, nothing is going to bring my mother back to life. Might as well let it go. Orpah's smart enough that she's gotten her cable show. She's got money, too; lots of lawyers at her disposal. If we accuse her of this, all she's got to do is sic her contacts on us, and that'll be the end of everything."

I bite back a sigh. "But you can ask Judge Piper for help in dealing with those things, can't you? He seems to be willing to stand up to her, and you, too."

"He's not family." Matthias snarls at me. "And neither are you. Why don't you just go back to Asher's room and wait for him? Let Sama have her spasms. If Mrs. Hennessey wasn't at the pie contest right now, I'd have her come and deal with her."

"She's your sister," I reply, angry he's every bit the tool I'd figured him to be.

"Half-sister," he corrects me.

"Fine." I put my hands on my hips. "*Half-sister.* But surely you don't think she's lying about something as important as this?"

"I know she is."

I cross my arms over my chest. "How?"

"Because *I* wasn't poisoned," Matthias snaps at me. "The other day I came here … I ate the same food as Mama did. And now she's dead. But I'm not."

Matthias holds up the bowl, as if to show me. "So even if Sama says she saw her put poison in here … "

His voice trails off as he looks at the bowl again.

"What is it?" I ask, more than annoyed with him.

"Nothing." Then he shakes his head. "Well, actually, this is the bowl Mama had the gravy in, and I don't eat gravy. But it's not like that would really change things … right?"

We exchange a look, and then we both look toward Sama's room.

As if Matthias can read my mind, he says, "But she's got Down's. No judge is going to listen to her testimony seriously."

I say nothing. I'd said too much in front of Asher about people with Down Syndrome, and I'm willing to bet I sounded even more awful then than Matthias does now.

"I'm sure she'd get to testify," I murmur. I mean, I don't actually know for sure, but … she was technically a witness to Orpah's visit. Maybe that would count for something.

Before Matthias can argue with me, there's a knock at the door.

I look down at myself, covered in flour and baking messes, and then I turn to Matthias expectantly. He rolls his eyes, but he saunters off to answer the door just like a grumpy teenager.

At that moment, my phone rings. I practically jump out of my ugly apron, but I hurriedly grab the phone and rejoice.

"Asher!" I gush as I answer the phone. "Where are you? What's going on? Sama and I are making tarts for everyone!"

"Pamela, I need you to come down to the festival," Asher says. "Judge Piper and I just finished talking with Officer McCain. It looks like there's probable cause for her to murder Mama."

"Well, of course there is!" I blurt out. "Sama told me she saw her poison her. She can testify, don't you think?"

Asher goes silent, and I wonder if he thinks I've gone crazy.

And maybe I have. Or maybe I was crazy before. It's hard to say, but hearing him talk to me again after the past few days of relative silence is so welcoming, and I don't want to mess this up.

So of course I'll probably mess it up.

"Just come to the festival," Asher says. "We're heading over now. The judge has to go give his pie contest verdict and he's going to watch Orpah get arrested. He's excited about it."

From Asher's voice, I know he's not. He seems scared, if anything.

I start taking off the apron; I will need a moment to clean up, and get dressed into something nicer, and I'll have to get Sama there, too. Matthias will have to drive, I realize with a grimace.

But dealing with Matthias is a small price to pay for being there for Asher.

"I'll be there soon," I promise.

"Thank you."

"I love you."

I say the words and hope to hear them back, but before I do, I hear Matthias and someone else's voice arguing in the front room. It's a man, and I don't recognize his voice.

I can't hear Asher's voice anymore, and I doubt he can hear me. The call cuts off, and I'm sad—no, I'm angry, and I head off to tell Matthias we're leaving.

"I got your money," Matthias is saying to the other man.

The other man would have looked nice, if it didn't look like he'd just come from a fistfight. He is wearing a business suit that's torn in some places; his lip is bloodied, and he has a black eye swelling up on his right side. There's a cut across his left eyebrow, giving him a dangerous look.

"What's going on?" I ask carefully, trying not to feel scared.

I feel like I'm walking into the middle of a drug exchange, and from Matthias' expression, I wonder if that's not entirely false.

I clear my throat. "Who is this?"

Matthias shuffles his feet. "This is my friend, Dennis."

"Dezmo," the man says, correcting Matthias. He nods to me. "Excuse me, ma'am. We're in the middle of a business discussion. We're sorry for the trouble. We'll take it outside."

Mrs. Hennessey would've been happy to see Dezmo's manners.

But I have other concerns.

"Asher just called," I tell Matthias. "We need to get to the pie contest as fast as possible. Asher and Judge Piper are waiting for us."

The two of them exchange a glance. Seeing their reluctance, I harden my glare.

This is too important.

I need them to cooperate. I need to take charge and get them to cooperate.

Finally, Dezmo shrugs. "That's okay with me, I guess; after the long car ride here, I could use some pie. Let's go. *And then* we can settle our business, MD."

Dezmo gives Matthias a warning look.

Matthias nods. "Alright, fine. I'll get Marjorie started up. But I don't want any trouble."

I exhale sharply, not even aware I'd been holding my breath. "Good. I'll get Sama."

"Ugh, I just said I don't want any trouble!"

"She has to come with us," I argue. "She'll be upset if we leave her here."

"She'll make a scene, or she'll just cause trouble."

I know, but I can't possibly worry about that. "I'll be there with her," I tell him. "And I'll let Sama know when we get back, I'll help her finish the apple tarts."

As the men head out the door and I put the tarts in the fridge, I feel my heart beat excitedly.

For the first time in days, I have hope—and I'm not going to let go of that.

HOMEMADE APPLE TARTS

A FEDUSKA FAMILY RECIPE

From the kitchen of Tabatha Feduska

HOMEMADE APPLE TARTS

Ingredients:

1 ½ cup + 1 TBSP all-purpose flour (you'll need more for dusting)

A nice pinch of kosher or pink Himalayan salt

12 TBSP (or a stick and a half) cold salted butter – place in freezer for 15 minutes before use

2 TBSP melted butter

1/3 cup ice water

3 ½ TBSP sugar (I tend to mound my sugar rather than level)

4 of your favorite apples (make sure they're large). I like

Jonathan, Jonagold, or Golden apples

2 TBSP apricot preserves, melted and strained

SECRET INGREDIENT: A squeeze of lemon

juice!

First, peel, core, and then cut apples into ¼ inch slices. It's easier to halve them before slicing.

Gently mix apples (with a squeeze or two of lemon) with about a tablespoon of sugar. Add more sugar if you like it sweeter.

For the crust …

Pulse 1 ½ cup flour and salt in a food processor.

Add in cold cubes of butter and pulse for 5-7 more seconds (it should be about the size of sweet peas).

Evenly sprinkle ice water in and pulse until it's moist.

Move the dough to a floured workspace and knead it until it is fully mixed.

Flatten into a nice circle that is about ¼ inch thick.

Get a baking sheet ready – I like to use parchment paper – and carefully transfer your dough circle to your baking sheet.

In a separate bowl, mix 2 TBSP of sugar with the 1 TBSP of flour you have left and then spread it evenly over the dough.

Place your apples in a spiraled circle. You don't want them right on the edge of the dough.

Start inward, and finish with about 3 or so inches left surrounding the apples.

Fold that dough up over the sides of the apples and brush it all with melted butter.

You should still have sugar left over from earlier: sprinkle that over your tart, but try not to get it on the parchment paper so it doesn't burn.

Chill the tart in the fridge for about 15 minutes while oven pre-heats to 400° F.

Bake at 400°F in the center of the oven for an hour or until tender (Love Me Tender♪) and your crust is golden. Once you've done that, you'll brush your melted apricot preserves onto your apples. Let it cool down for a bit and then serve.

Optional: serve with homestyle vanilla ice cream

from
TABATHA FEDUSKA

"For my family, cooking has always meant lots of heart-to-hearts, laughter, shenanigans, and lots of love. Let's not forget the deliciousness that comes out of our kitchen as a result.

"Baking and cooking have always been a way to unwind, make sweet memories, and bring us together. It's funny how smells and tastes of our favorite family foods can take us back to a special place and time, like music does. We recall our Grandmomma's famed

banana pudding and the joy her smiles brought. How my mom's fried squash has become a birthday staple. My Granddaddy's bourbon pecan pie. Mine and my oldest daughter's secret snickerdoodles. All of these things warm my heart.

"Being in the kitchen surrounded by the ones we love is what it's all about to me. The ones that have passed on before us and their special recipes and their loving memories we pass on to our own kiddos. My kiddos. We create new memories – and messes to go along with them – to pass on down the line. Our love for baking and cooking and our love for those around us and in our hearts all meet together in the kitchen and around the table where we enjoy each other and the food before us."

PIE GUY

AN OUTSIDER GETS AN INSIDE LOOK

Life of Pies, Book 9

C. S. Johnson

CHAPTER NINE
Dennis "Dezmo" Moreland

When I was young, my pa told me something that often comes to mind, as if my old man's ghost is just itching to whisper in my ear.

He used to say, "Whenever someone criticizes you, just remember all the people in the world don't gotta deal with the disadvantages you do. So no matter what they say, you don't owe them jack shit, unless you're fool enough to believe it."

Pa had his flaws as a man, God rest his soul, but I have to admit, he had a solid point.

I especially wonder this as I sit in the passenger seat of MD's old car, while his Down Syndrome half-sister and his brother's girlfriend are in the backseat, and we're on our way to a pie contest.

A pie contest, of all things!

And this is after I'd just driven for hours, following a solid scuff-up with a couple of stock-jock loan sharks itching for their payday.

Maybe they'd knocked the sense out of me.

"Thanks for coming, man," MD mutters out of the corner of his mouth. I know he doesn't want the girls to overhear us. He lets out a small sigh. "Sorry I bailed on you before."

"*You're* sorry?" I scoff. "Well, yeah, I'm sorry, too. I'm sorry that Jack Garlin's got his men on our scent, and they found me before they found you."

"I'll make it up to you."

I cross my arms. "You'd better. You're already wasting my time as it is."

"You know, you didn't *have to* come. You could've waited till I got back. Pie contest'll be done in an hour or so," MD grumbles.

"I get that the women want to go. I mean, it's pie," I say, nodding slightly toward the backseat. "But why are *we* going there?"

MD shrugs. "Damned if I know."

"Damned if I know why I haven't thrown you under the bus yet, either. You're friggin' nuts, man."

A sharp pain hits me from the back of my seat; behind me, MD's little sister wiggles around while the girlfriend is trying to get her to sit still.

I give the girlfriend an irritated look, but she's wide-eyed with helplessness.

Not used to dealing with the mentally challenged, I see.

I smirk at the thought. *Wonder how she's going to deal with MD?*

The rest of the ride passes by in relative silence, with the exception of the Down Syndrome girl. She makes some slurping sounds as we go through Main Street. If she had been a four year old instead of a teenage girl, it might've been more appropriate.

Already, I feel like an outsider for sure. The Fairmont Spring Festival is in full, southern spirit mode. The town is all dolled up like a Southern-Bell-styled hooker. Businesses have flags and posters and plenty of signs out, offering discounts and trying to shill their stuff. All around us are people in their flannel shirts and jeans, and some sweaters, all while I'm in a slightly-bloodied suit.

MD focuses on the road in front of us. "Sama, get buckled and stay buckled, or so help me God I will stop the car and kick you out!"

"Matthias," the girlfriend objects. "That's not very nice."

"Neither's dying by getting thrown out of the car!"

The girlfriend pouts, and I have to admit, I can see why MD's bro would've picked her up. Her lips are full and red and tempting; they clash well with her bright red hair.

I'd tap that, too.

We pull into a crowded parking lot, and after going up and down several rows, we finally fins a space.

We squeeze out of the car and head toward the entrance.

I feel like I'm walking onto a horror movie set, one of the old ones, where all the black people are the first to die.

"Maybe I should stay in the car," I say, feeling uneasy as I look around. Honestly, it's not that different from what MD and I do for Nashville's music business, but we work the virtual fields.

That was how MD and I got started in stock management funds—checking out new artists and using them as investment pools.

And that's also the reason I had to drive for hours to get here, I remind myself.

"You can stay if you want." MD jerks his thumb toward the girls. "I'll go with them to find Asher."

I frown at his surly tone. "If you just give me the money, I can leave altogether."

"I said I got it," MD hisses, shooting me a quick glare. "There's just other stuff to take care of first."

"What could be more important than saving our skins? I told you we shouldn't have offered Jack any extra margins. Not when Galinda Daystar managed to catch pneumonia and mono in the same week."

"We'll get the money back," MD reminds me. "Her concert'll sell out four times, even if we need a few more weeks."

"The hype will be gone, man."

"We'll have to manufacture the hype, then."

"That'll sink us in even more."

"Nah. We know what we're doing. Jack just needs to sit tight for a bit."

"He wants his money back, now." I gesture down the front of my shirt, where there is still some dried blood from earlier. My nose had been punched in real good, but I took the punch like a man; Pa would've approved. "If you haven't noticed."

"I noticed."

"Asher!" The girlfriend cheers up considerably as she points to a man up ahead. Even from this distance, I can tell he's related to MD; he has the similar coloring, same brooding stare.

As if he hears us, Asher looks back toward our small group. He's certainly confused, but he nudges the man standing next to him—an older gentleman, dressed in proper pants and a vest—and then he heads over our way.

"Pip." The Down's girl behind me seems excited, and she skips off.

"Sama, wait for me," the girlfriend says, following after her.

MD keeps his pace, clearly disinterested.

Again, I have to wonder why we were even here.

"Hey." MD nods toward another man. "That's Garland Morris. He's my mama's banker."

"So?" I hiss. "Is *he* going to give us the money we need to get Jack off our back?"

"Maybe." MD frowns. "Let's go talk to him."

This Garland Morris guy is practically sweating bullets as MD approaches him.

"Mr. Morris," MD greets him. "Nice to see you again, sir."

The man looks MD up and down. "I'm surprised you recognized me. Martha's shown me a few of your photographs over the years, God bless her."

"I've actually been trying to get a hold of you regarding my mama," MD continues. "She gave me a check before she died. Any chance you'll know if she's good for it. She did say you've taken good care of her all these years."

Morris wipes his forehead off with a handkerchief. "Not now, Matthias. I'm off the clock, and I've been feeling under the weather. If I hadn't been selected as one of the judges for the pie contest, I wouldn't even have come this year. I don't even care if your mother's pie is here." He looks toward the ground. "It won't be the same now that she's gone, too."

"That's how Judge Piper feels," MD grumbles. He continues to pry the banker with questions, but the man seems unwilling to talk.

I look around, irritated and impatient.

That's when I see her.

"Oh my God," I yelp, slapping MD on the shoulder. "Look! It's Orpah Abraham!"

MD groans. "Of course it's her. She's always here at the pie festival."

Morris mutters something unintelligible behind me, but I'm just in awe.

"MD, let's see if she'll host Galinda on her talk show," I say. "We're close enough to her I can reach out and touch her cornrows."

"She's not going to agree to it," MD says.

"Come on, you didn't even try!" I want to shake him. "Don't you see? If we tell Jack that Orpah's interested in an interview, he might not pull out his investment. We're in the clear!"

"We'll be in the clear anyway, after Morris here tells me about my mama's money," MD hisses, turning back to face the banker.

Morris shakes his head. "Not now, Matthias. This is just plain rude, anyway. Your mama wouldn't appreciate this. Have a little faith, won't you?"

He pushes MD out of his way, and he walks over toward the pie judging table.

There are more people heading over, too, and I figure it must be time for the judging to start.

I see this as my chance. I glance at MD. "I'm going to go talk to her before everyone else gets there," I say. "If you're not going to help me, I'm just going to help myself."

"Dez, come on—"

But I don't listen to MD. Honestly, the man's smart and he's been one of my best friends, but personal dignity has a price, and if he's not willing to pay for mine, I don't know if we were ever really friends.

"Hold up right there."

A new voice calls out, and the crowd uniformly turns to see a cop holding up a pair of handcuffs.

The whispers take off like wildfire through an oil field.

Even MD goes still behind me.

I glance over at him sideways. "You think we should get out of here, maybe?"

He says nothing, but as I watch, the police officer walks right up to me.

My palms are suddenly clammy, and I feel like I'm going to be sick. MD and I don't have anything *really* illegal going on, but who knows what Jack Garlin might've said back in Nashville? And who really could know how vast his underground empire is?

The police officer looks me over with a quick frown, but then he walks right on by me.

I swear I'm going to vomit.

But pure shock takes hold of me again, as the officer stops in front of Orpah Abraham herself.

The ebony goddess of daytime TV looks up at him and smiles, her famous gap-toothed grin welcoming and awe-inspiring.

"There you are, Officer McCain," she purrs. "Are you here to announce the winners?"

"No." The middle-aged, milksop of a police man heaves a rueful sigh. "Orpah Abraham, I'm sorry, but I have a signed warrant here, along with evidence."

Orpah's pleasantly round, colorful face scrunches up and darkens at once. I can't seem to stop staring as she points her long-tipped nailed finger at the man beside Asher. "If Judge Piper signed the warrant, he is corrupt. There's a clear conflict of interest, given how he's hated me over the years! I want my lawyer!"

The man I presume to be Judge Piper steps forward.

"Even if I was the one to sign the warrant, every person here knows I have picked your pies over everyone else's for the last twelve years."

"That was a matter of taste," Orpah shoots back. "This is about murder!"

Judge Piper, Garland Morris, and Officer McCain all exchange a surprised look.

"No one said anything about murder," Officer McCain tells her.

Orpah flushes over, clearly upset. "Well, that's just because that's what this is, isn't it?" Her hands are shaking as she tears at the warrant's envelope.

All of us are watching, breathless.

Even I'm shocked.

Did she just confess to murder?

Asher's girlfriend steps forward with the sister all of a sudden.

"Yes, it *is* murder; Sama saw you, and she can testify in court! I looked it up, even though she has Down Syndrome."

"Pamela," Asher hisses, clearly embarrassed.

The girlfriend—Pamela—blushes but she stands firm. "Well, Sama told me that Orpah did it, Asher. Matthias, you heard her, too."

I watch MD cringe as everyone else turns to look at him.

Lucky for him, Orpah doesn't seem to enjoy losing the spotlight, even if it's a negative one.

"This is asinine, and illegal," she hollers. "We all know you're just trying to bring me down. You're so grief-stricken over Martha's murder—I mean, death—that you'd blame me!"

Officer McCain steps up beside her. "Miss Abraham, let's roll down to the station and talk through things while we get you processed."

"Processed?" Orpah gasps. "This is outrageous, Solomon. I can't believe that you are doing this to me, too. You know I wouldn't murder anyone. Why, I'm not even capable of lying."

He looks at her for a long moment, while the rest of us remain transfixed at the scene.

"What about your assistant?" Officer McCain asks. "Would she lie?"

"Never to you," Orpah says. "She can tell you that I'm innocent. Shanae, come here."

A young lady—who is absolutely gorgeous, by the way—walks up to the policeman. He asks her a quiet question, and she looks down at the ground.

"What did she say?" Someone else from the crowd yells from behind me, and I look to see another crazy-eyed kind of lady.

"Calm down, Clarice," an annoyed man calls back. "He asked her where she threw out the package Orpah's pie came in."

The crowd collectively gasps, and I'm lost.

"What's that mean?" I ask MD. "Most pies come in a pan, right?"

"She apparently bought a pie for the contest," MD mutters. He must see the look of confusion my face, because he further explains, "A store-bought pie, not a homemade one. It's against the rules."

"So this is bad?"

"Yes."

"But it's a pie," I remind him. "Orpah Abraham can't get arrested for a fake pie, can she?"

"People here are probably more concerned with the pie," MD says cynically. "And if Sama wasn't lying, Orpah probably did kill my mama."

"Oprah Abraham killed your mom?" I rub my forehead. "Shit, man, I thought growing up in Chicago was hard. But why would she do something like that?"

MD shrugs. "I'm not sure. Probably over the pies, by the sound of it."

All around us, the people start arguing over each other. Some women are literally weeping, upset at the idea that Orpah Abraham has been faking her pies for the last twelve years. Others cry out, outraged that Orpah is being unfairly maligned.

"How dare you do this to my Martha," Judge Piper's voice booms out as he steps forward. "We have the proof you had access to the poison, we know you had

the chance to do it, and now we know for sure you've been faking your pies, Orpah."

"You can't prove anything," Orpah yells back, furious. "You're a racist old man who loves his white woman whore more than any sense of justice. You would side with me if you knew how Martha belittled me."

"She didn't 'belittle' you; she was the one who made your pies," Judge Piper shoots back. "And you ought to know not to call her a whore—not after what your brother did to her. He paid her off. The bank records confirm it, just like they confirm you're the one paying the bills for the punk kid I just sentenced to life for killing his neighbor. He used hemlock and ricin, too."

Officer McCain stands between them. "We have the confirmation on the autopsy, too, Miss Abraham. As I said, we can go to the station, or we can keep having a full-blown yelling contest for the whole community to hear!" He looks around. "What would you prefer?"

"I'd prefer my lawyer on the line," Orpah says, jerking out her cell phone, as she slowly follows Officer McCain to his car. Orpah turns to Shelly, her assistant. "You're fired, by the way."

There are more tears to be shed—first by Shelly, or Shirley, or whatever her name is, then by the people in the crowd who are upset Orpah has been framed and set up by Judge Piper, her assistant, her charity, her brother, or just "the system."

Further up by the pie stand, I watch as Asher gives Pamela a small kiss on the cheek, while Sama leans on her other side. Judge Piper is shaking hands with Morris, and even MD smiles.

"Well, she'll probably still get away with it. She's rich, after all," he says. His voice breaks a little, and I realize he's trying not to cry, but he wants to play it cool. "But it's nice to see the court of public opinion is still going to punish her somewhat."

The celebration and despair around us finally settles down a little, and Judge Piper calls out, "Well, who is ready to judge some pies?"

Half the crowd cheers, while the other half slowly slinks away, headed for other parts of the festival, or maybe even just heading home.

"You're biased against Orpah," one of the ladies calls out. "You shouldn't be a judge this year. Especially since Martha's last pie is in the competition."

Judge Piper looks at her thoughtfully. "Mrs. Montgomery, perhaps you're right. Morris and I should step down. Who can we get to judge though, who's not biased?"

MD laughs as he pushes me up front. "Here's my friend Dez," he calls. "Make him do it."

"What are you doing?" I snap. "I don't want to be no pie judge."

"Just do it," MD says. "Then I'll give you my mama's check, okay? And then you can leave."

He pulls out a small, folded check out of his pocket. I don't know if it's real, but I'm tired of dealing with all this pie contest shit.

"Fine," I agree reluctantly.

After I clear my throat, I stand up to face the crowd. "I'm an outsider. I don't know anyone other than Orpah, and I'm assuming her pie's being disqualified anyway."

"Perfect! I hope you like plum pie!" the lady who'd called out Judge Piper smiles brightly at me.

"That's the banker's wife," MD mutters behind me. "I remember her making terrible pies from even before Orpah started entering."

I'm handed an apron to cover up my suit, and then a fork. And then I'm given a small tray, full of plates, each presented with a sliver from twelve different pies.

I glance back at MD, and the others, and then shake my head.

Everyone is waiting.

So I take careful bites.

Some of them are delicious. Others are much less so.

I personally don't see what the big allure is, but all the pie makers are standing around. The closest thing I can think of as a comparison is some kind of televised dog show for rich white ladies.

The man who I assume is the mayor follows after me, taking several more bites than I do, although he's clearly enjoying the contest vastly more than I am.

"Tell us what you think is the best," Judge Piper says. "Mr. … ?"

"Uh, Mr. Moreland," I answer. "But you can call me Dez."

"Alright, Mr. Dez," Judge Piper says. "Which pie do you think is the best?"

"Well, it's definitely not the plum pie," I murmur. I must've said it more loudly than I'd meant to, because a lady standing next to another old man in a suit starts crying into her hanky. She's the one who'd said she hoped I liked plum, so it makes sense that she's the one who would cry.

I'd cry too, if I made pie this poorly. And I don't even bake.

As if sensing a good photo-opt and sound-bite, the mayor cuts me off. "Well, I think they're all spectacular this year, and I'm so, so sad I only get to vote for one. But I think the lemon meringue has my vote, for sure!"

"I'll agree to that," I say.

The mayor, for all his brown-nosing, is right; the lemon meringue was definitely the best out of the lot.

I record my vote, take the apron off, put the fork down, and head back over to MD.

"Well?" I ask, holding out my hand. "Give me the check."

MD shrugs. "Fine."

Before he can give it to me, however, the lady who'd spoken up before, Clarice, steps up to the front.

"Wait," she says. "We still need one more outsider to judge. If Morris is resigning, it can't be just the mayor with this guy."

There's a small round of silence, and then another man walks forward.

He's an older man, pale, with dark grey eyes that look clouded with grief and toil. He's wearing non-descript clothes, and there's a cigarette in his right hand that looks just about gone.

I feel almost bad for him. He seems like a lonely person, although I don't know why I feel that way.

The man clears his throat. "I'll be a judge, if that's okay with everyone."

Beside me, MD goes still. His eyes are wide, and his jaw is slack with disbelief.

"Papa?"

At the moment, MD is my friend again, and I decide it's best that we go; I know what I would do if my old man showed up out of nowhere like this.

I nudge MD's shoulder. "Come on, let's go."

MD slowly shakes his head. "No. I gotta stay for a bit."

I know there's more he wants to say; something about family, probably, with his mother's death or murder, and now his father's return.

But it's not a conversation for me, and as far as I'm concerned, money talks louder right now.

"Well, I'm outta here," I say, snatching the check out from between MD's fingers. I look around uneasily; this is definitely not where I belong. "I'll get a ride to the house somehow. See you later, man. Sorry for all the crazy trouble you've had to deal with."

MD doesn't seem to hear me. He and his brother are too busy staring at his would-be dad. Everyone else has gone silent, too.

I walk away, feeling relieved. As I head toward the exit, I take the moment to remind myself I'm not rich enough to get away with murder, fame can make you do crazy pie stuff, and being an outsider can be a good thing when insane shit goes down.

They can all sort it out without me, I decide.

Anyway, I don't owe them anything, really. I've already taken a beaten for MD. And now, I've gotten what I came for.

I smile, as I hold up the check and whistle at the large number on it.

I've gotten my money, and I've gotten some good compensation, too, if I count all the free pie.

That is all nice, but it is even sweeter to head home.

CHERRY PIE

A PIATT FAMILY RECIPE

From the kitchen of Tascha Piatt

CHERRY PIE

Ingredients:

2 pie crusts

2 LBS frozen, pitted cherries – thawed with juices (preferable dark, sweet cherries)

1/3 cup granulated sugar

2 TBSP cornstarch

¼ cup water

Pinch of salt (about ¼ TSP)

Splash of lime juice, optional (about ½ TSP)

1 egg + 1 TBSP water, beaten for egg wash

Optional: 1 TBSP sugar, for sprinkling

Prepare bottom crust in 9" deep-dish pie pan; set

aside top crust.

Preheat oven to 350°

In large saucepan, stir cornstarch into water.

Over low heat, add sugar, stirring constantly until

sugar is fully dissolved.

Add thawed cherries and all juices, and stir to coat with water mixture.

Sprinkle in salt (and lime juice, if adding) and stir once more.

Carefully pour into prepared pie dish.

Add top crust, either flat with center slices or latticed, carefully sealing all edges.

Brush with egg wash and sprinkle with extra sugar if desired.

Cover loosely with foil and bake for 20 minutes.

Remove foil and bake for an additional 45-50 minutes or until crust is set and inside is

bubbly (I like to check at 35-40 minutes).

Best if allowed to set 2-3 hours before serving.

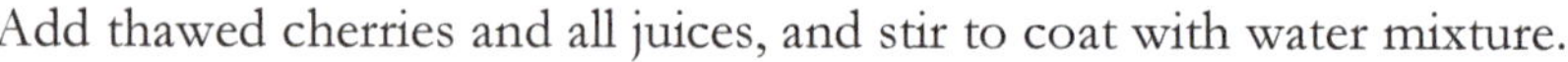

from
TASCHA PIATT

"I cook, and sometimes even bake, flying by the seat of my pants. This recipe is completely from memory – none of my recipes are written.

"The first time I made cherry pie was because my parents were coming to visit, and it is one of my dad's favorite pies. I had recently discovered I do like cherries (I had only ever had those jarred cherries or canned pie filling, and thought they were not pleasant).

"Now cherry pie is one of my favorites, too, when made this way."

MY PEACH OF THE PIE

A STRANGER COMES BACK HOME

Life of Pies, Book 10

C. S. Johnson

CHAPTER TEN

Joe Davidson

The world is a strange place, and even stranger when it's full of familiar strangers.

A sense of disoriented déjà vu permeates me as I stare around the Fairmont Spring Festival, looking in wonder at my would-be, once-were neighbors.

It's been fifteen years since I've come back into town. As I watch faces flicker with vague recognition or apathetic dismissal, I suddenly feel every minute of that decision.

Raw grief, and then relief, staggers through me, accompanied by a sense that even though I deserve to feel this low, I'll still take it over the suffering I would've been subjected to if I'd stayed.

Honestly, I don't even know why I came back at all.

It's just then I see my oldest son's face through the crowd; maybe I had been expecting to see him, or even been hoping to.

Looking at him now, I still don't know.

Maybe my eyes are just playing tricks on me, too.

I study the man carefully, inconspicuously. He's looking on at the Pie Queen contest, and his jaw is clenched as he's spitting out short, stagnated comments to the man in the suit beside him. He looks a lot like Martha, from what I remember of her, and after a moment, I can only shake my head.

I take a long inhale of the cigarette I started in the car, feeling like a drowning man tasting air above the water.

Damned if I know why.

A woman sniffles off to the side of me. "Martha would've loved the pie contest this year, bless her heart."

The woman's comment makes me flinch. It's almost like a sign, and a confirmation that I've been cursed.

Not that Martha would've cursed me—no, she was too sweet for her own good.

Or so anyone else would've thought.

I know the *real* truth.

She was a saint, alright—the kind that would always shame you for being less than worthy of her presence.

And then she went to that conference about baking and cooking, and wound up hooking up with my best friend.

Oh, sure, she insisted that it wasn't her fault, and that she'd been assaulted and raped and demeaned by Omar, and all those things women like to say after they've done wrong.

But when I confronted Omar about it, he told me the truth.

He'd said Martha was only too grateful for the attention; that I'd been neglecting her sexual needs, that I wasted our income on booze and drugs, and that I even spent too much time hanging out with Omar as he and his sister tried getting their political campaigns off the ground. And, Omar insisted, he'd been there with his sister, Orpah, and she could vouch for him. And she did; she told me herself that Martha was just as eager as anyone else to get ahold of her clout, and that she'd willingly seduced her brother the first time the opportunity presented itself.

That was back when Orpah didn't have such a big following, too.

As if on a cue, that's when I hear Orpah's voice.

"This is outrageous!"

I glance back up, no longer caught up in my past. I watch as Orpah tries to shrug off the police chief. I can hear her mumble something about racism and sexism, and how her life is ruined.

"Ms. Abraham, you needn't make this any harder than it has to be," the policeman says as they head toward me.

"Oh, hell no," she spits back. "I'll make this as hard for you as I can. *I'm* the victim here, if you haven't noticed!"

"From the looks of it, Martha Davidson is the victim here," the policeman says back, clearly disappointed.

I flinch at the mention of my ex-wife.

"Oh, great," Orpah snaps. "Joe's here."

She's seen me.

I try not to flinch again as I meet her cold gaze. "Hello, Orpah."

She pauses here, pushing back on the policeman who's holding her arm. "Well, well, well. If it isn't the money-grubbing man himself I see. Tell me, have you come to claim Martha's money for your own?"

I'm shocked she's even talking to me, but why she'd mention money is beyond me.

"Excuse me?" I ask, not sure what to say.

"Oh, don't play dumb," Orpah snaps. "You're probably really happy she's gone, huh? Now you can claim all of Omar's payoff for yourself. Unless that judge has managed to write you out of all of it, huh?"

She nods back toward the pie contest where a new judge is tasting a bunch of the different pie slices. I don't know who she's talking about it, but I doubt it's that guy. He looks too simple-minded to be a man of the law, and if it weren't for the pies, he likely wouldn't even be here at all.

Hardly a local, I think, as I take another long inhale from my cigarette.

The heat burns down into my lungs, and it kindles something resembling bravery as I shrug at Orpah.

"I don't know, Orpah," I say. "I just got the message she'd passed and I came here out of nothing but a sense of morbid curiosity."

Orpah sizes me up with the same old shrewd look on her face. "Well, you're as useless as you've always been, then. Omar was right to cut ties with you. You're a loser, Joe. A poor-minded loser who's always chasing the next buck while he's spending the last ten."

That stings, and more than expected.

"Well, with all due respect, Ms. Abraham, I'm not the one getting arrested." I nod to the police officer, who seems to take this as his cue to leave.

"I'll see you in hell!" Orpah yells back at me. "And Martha, too!"

I can hear the policeman groan softly. "Please, Orpah; if you're not guilty, you'll get everything back that's owed to you."

"Ha! I'll never get back my good name!"

I roll my eyes and turn back to the pie contest.

I have to admit, it's not every day that Orpah Abraham gets arrested. And while that's not the reason I came back to Fairmont, I have to admit, it's a nice bonus.

I already had no more goodwill left for Omar, and I'm happy to have none for Orpah, either. I wrote off the Abraham family a long time ago, but it is nice to see some kind of real-world karma catch up with them.

Even if Martha had to die for it.

I pause, running Orpah's words over in my mind again.

Does she really think Martha only had money because of Omar?

I shrug again and start walking up toward the pie contest table.

I'm hungry, and once the pie contest is finished, they cut up the rest of the pies to make samples for the audience.

As I come forward, people are chatting together about Martha and Orpah, but I just focus on the pies.

They all look so neat and tidy up on their table. Looking at them, I'd never normally guess the lies and desperation behind them.

But they are really pretty.

That lady earlier had been right. Martha would have liked this.

She'd always been good at baking, and pies were her specialty. She used to make me the best pies, especially her peach pie.

I walk up next to the display, watching as the mayor and the pie guy do their judging.

I don't see any peach pie, and suddenly I feel sad.

Almost like I thought there should be something there, and it wasn't.

My heart suddenly aches.

When Martha found out she was pregnant, and she didn't want to abort the baby, and she didn't want to bring up charges against Omar for sexual assault, it was then I knew Omar had been telling the truth.

He'd even said she would deny their affair.

He'd said she would try to frame him as the bad guy.

He'd said she felt wracked with guilt and anger, and it was all from her own sense of regret that she had to go back home with her children and try to smooth it over with me.

What kind of wife would ask her husband to raise another man's child?

After discovering the truth, I saved up enough money to leave and get as far away from her as possible, and I never looked back.

Not until today.

I look around again, happy I'd left.

These people are all whispering about Orpah, and they are happy to believe the worst in her. If I'd've stayed, they would've done the same thing, only with me.

They probably even did after I left, saying that Martha had been assaulted, and forced to raise her rapist's baby, all while I left.

Martha wasn't a subject I liked to think about much. Over the years, I'd been happy to forget about her as I worked job after job, trying to keep myself afloat and free.

"We need a new judge," a lady says, just off to my right. "Morris has to resign. He's compromised by this Martha and Orpah situation, too."

"But they're not even counting Orpah's pie," another man says. "Her assistant more or less admitted it wasn't Orpah's."

"That's her assistant saying that," the lady argues. "What if it's all been a set up?"

"Orpah's not exactly pristine," someone else says. "She's probably not innocent. I'd be surprised if Martha was the first person she murdered."

"You're just saying that because she's black!"

I roll my eyes, and then take another long draw from my cigarette. It's all the way gone, and now I want some sugar.

"I'll be a judge, if that's okay with everyone."

I step forward, positioning myself before them, and I swear I'd forgotten all about my son being there.

And there is my other son, too, I realize. Asher is here, just as Matthias is. I see him standing with an older black man, a redheaded beauty, and a teenage girl with large, wide-set eyes and curly black hair.

All of them are looking at me, and I suddenly feel embarrassed again; I've gotten so used to ignoring my sons that it's more natural to keep forgetting them.

But then, when I left, I hadn't been thinking about Martha, or my sons; I'd only been thinking of my own desperately wounded pride.

I straighten my shoulders, trying to shrug off the sudden pain in my chest. "Well?"

"He's a stranger," someone else says. "He's the perfect judge for this!"

"He's not a stranger," someone else retorts. "He used to live here!"

"No."

Matthias speaks up at last, and I turn to see the other pie-guy judge shift away from him and then turn around and run.

"No, no one knows this guy," Matthias says.

"Matthias!" Asher shouts. "That's our father."

"No," Matthias shakes his head. "No, he's not."

His words are likely designed to hurt me, but my son doesn't know I'm used to it. He doesn't really have a way to hurt me.

The older black man clears his throat. "Just let him judge the pies. He'll be objective enough. Won't you, sir?"

I nod, more confident than ever. "I'm more than capable of that, Mister."

It's nice to just move through the pies, even if people are watching me. I'm given a scorecard, and I check off things like "looks evenly baked," "no burn marks" and "good amount of filling."

I move from one end with the plum pie, the cherry pie, the blueberry pie, a couple of apple ones, and even a pineapple and apple one; none of them are particularly memorable, taste-wise, until I come to the lemon meringue.

Tasting it, all my memories I'd locked up suddenly come bursting free.

I think of the first time Martha baked a pie for me.

I feel younger, as I see her younger self, too, as she holds out the pie to me.

It's for our picnic—our first date.

My hands grow warm as I hold onto the pan. I put it down carefully, and then she cuts me a slice. I resist for a moment, but she gives me a bite off her fork.

"It's peach," she says to me, laughing as I feel genuinely moved by the experience.

"This is … wonderful," I manage to choke out, feeling like I was in the presence of an angel.

I'm too moved to speak. Her eyes are bright and shining and full of excitement, and I feel like the only man in the world as she watches me.

"The secret ingredient is love," she whispers, and before I can stop myself, I'm leaning over to kiss her.

She tastes of peaches and sweetness, and it's at that moment I fall in love.

Shortly after that, I vow I will marry her.

My eyes blink, and I find myself in the present moment again.

The memories are gone as I put the lemon meringue slice down. It is my last piece, and it carries an aftertaste of bittersweet salt, and I can only be glad when I realize I'm not crying.

How did it come to this?

I see Martha's smiling face after she pulls away from our first kiss.

Back then, she made me feel a way that only a woman in love can make a man feel.

Knowing how it ends scorches me—it makes my heart twist in anger and self-disgust.

How did it come to this end?

I feel the assurance in Martha's hand as I put her ring on her finger, and we vow before God, community, and family, that we will love each other and stay true to each other until death do we part.

The future had seemed so bright and so full ...

I can see Martha's painful joy as she gives birth to Matthias.

The present can't be farther away from what it was supposed to be ...

I look back at my sons, standing behind me at the pie contest. They look at me, and I go back to ignoring them.

This day was never meant to be like this …

I think of Martha bringing Asher home, as Matthias rides on my shoulders.

I fall into a heated memory of cigar smoke and whiskey, a haze of arguments and screams; I see myself getting laid off from my job; I feel myself handing over money for more alcohol, more food, more cigarettes; I see myself walking away, drunk on a dirt road, ashamed and alone.

I see Martha's smiling memory fade away into the dark.

Carefully, I put the pie down.

"The lemon meringue has my vote," I hear myself say.

Immediately, the nearby crowd cheers.

"It's Martha's pie!" a lady says, and I see her gaze past me. "Edith, did you hear? Martha's pie won!"

"Really?" The woman's face seems familiar as I look over at her. Both of the women are suddenly crying as they race over to hug each other.

I wonder if they'd bet money on it or something.

"Martha who?" I ask, although I already suspect I know the answer.

"Martha Davidson," a nearby man says to me. "It's the last pie she ever made, you know. She and Orpah were legends in this town."

"Were they?"

"Yeah," the man continues. "I think it's a shame Martha died, though. You know she was going to get married to Judge Piper over there? He's there standing with her daughter."

I don't bother glancing over again. I already feel like I don't belong here—and I don't, really.

The man doesn't realize I'm eager to get away.

"I don't know what we'll do now, with Martha gone and Orpah off to jail."

"I see."

I shrug. "Time to find a new legend, I guess."

I put down the plate, and I look at the pie carefully; I don't know why, but I don't feel the same way about Martha's pie as I used to. Perhaps it's because the love she'd had for me is gone, now, too.

As the mayor announces the winner and two women hurry forward to collect the prize in Martha's honor, I look over at Matthias. He turns away from me.

But Asher doesn't.

He sees me and heads over, and it's my turn to decide if I should stay or go again.

I turn away; he shouldn't have to deal with me, not after all these years.

"Papa, wait."

Asher grabs my arm, and I reluctantly turn to face him.

"I think you're mistaken," I say carefully.

"I think you're mistaken," he says. "Matthias and I know it's you, even if he doesn't want to say anything. But I do."

I swallow hard. "Well, get it over with."

He nods, and then he opens his mouth.

I prepare for the worst, but then he closes it.

"I don't really know what to say," he explains a moment later. "I never thought I'd see you again. I'm hurt, but I'm happy to see you're alive, too."

Martha's passing had to have been hard on him, I realize.

I nod. "I understand."

"Asher." The redheaded lady comes up beside him and takes his arm. She's followed by the teenager with the wide-set eyes, and I don't have to guess that this is the baby I'd asked Martha to abort.

Asher is surprised, but the redheaded lady nods toward me. "Are you going to introduce me?"

"Oh. Right." He's not eager to do so, but it's no matter; without prodding, the lady reaches out and shakes my hand. "Pamela, this is my father."

"And this is your wife?" I assume.

"Well, no," Pamela admits with an embarrassed blush. "I'm his girlfriend. And this is Sama."

She wraps her hand companionably in the girl's, and I'm touched to see that the two of them appear to be friends.

Sama doesn't say anything as she looks at me, and the rest of us are quiet.

"Thanks for coming," Asher finally says.

"Don't thank him," Matthias' voice cuts through the air, as if drawing a line between us. "He probably just came back for the money."

"What money?" I ask, unable to help myself.

"The five hundred thousand that Omar used to pay her off," the man I'd been talking to earlier says.

Omar?

I look over at him. "Who are you, again?"

"I'm Morris, her banker," the man explains, taking another bite of Martha's pie.

"Yes, Mama gave me the money before she died, and I gave it away already," Matthias says. "So you're not getting anything."

I look at them all over again—my oldest son, my younger son, their half-sister, and the girlfriend.

It hits me, sudden and hard, that maybe I'd been wrong about Martha after all.

Maybe she wasn't lying … maybe.

It's hard to know what to believe, after all this time. Even if it's true, all the very worst of it … even if Martha had been raped, even if Omar had been lying to me, even if he'd had pleasure in taking what was mine and destroying it for his own game, even if Orpah had lied to me … nothing changes the fact that Martha kept the baby and did nothing to press charges …

But she was paid off … the banker just said so!

No, I tell myself. That doesn't change anything.

Doesn't it?

No. It doesn't. I still left, and I still wouldn't be shamed by raising my wife's baby with another man.

I look at the two young men before me, seeing more of my own face in them.

I still left them.

I still hurt them.

"I guess you can leave now," Matthias says. "Now that you know you're not welcome here."

I'm grateful that he's shocked me out of my thoughts—nothing truly did change the past.

The result is the same: I'd left Fairmont so many years before, and I had nothing left.

And now, I have more than nothing left; even if I apologize and truly regret leaving them, I have nothing to offer them in regards to the future.

Martha is dead, and so am I. My body is just still alive in the meantime.

Slowly, I nod. "Yes," I agree. "It was … nice seeing you."

No one says anything, and once more, I turn away.

But then, once more, another hand reaches out and grabs me.

"Wait." It's the girlfriend this time. "Martha's funeral is tomorrow. You should come to that."

"Pamela," Matthias hisses, clearly upset, while Asher just looks on in confusion. "It's not like he cares. He's never cared. Otherwise, he would've never left. Just let him leave—again."

"No," Pamela says quietly. "No, people can change, Matthias. We've all made mistakes, and sometimes we don't know how to make up for them. If we can at all. But we should still try."

She looks up at me again, and I have to give Asher credit; she's a real beauty, and clearly very smart. She might even be trying to manipulate me—and I am almost happy she's good enough at it for me to fall for it.

"You do want to come, don't you? To say goodbye properly?"

She asks this with expectation in her voice, and I feel myself slowly nod. "Alright," I say. "I'll be there tomorrow."

"Good." She gestures around the festival. "Well, now that the pie contest is over, we should check out the rest of the festival. What do you say, Sama?"

Sama shakes her head as she leans on Pamela's shoulders. "No," Sama says. "I want to go home and finish my apple tarts."

Her voice reminds me of Martha. As Pamela tries to convince Sama to look around the fair first, I turn back to my sons.

I still don't know what to say; I start to wish I had another cigarette.

"I'm sorry about your mother."

It's not what I think I really wanted to say, but it's the truth. I am sorry about Martha's death—and I'm sorry I wasn't there for them when they were younger.

Perhaps if I had been, I wouldn't feel so lousy now.

It's at this moment that Asher hugs me.

I'm more than surprised by his display of affection, and I hold on and pat his back.

I don't want to let go.

I'm genuinely touched by his kindness, and my eyes start to water.

Matthias is harder than his brother; he scowls at me as Asher lets me go.

"We'll see you tomorrow," he mutters. "Don't do anything to embarrass us, alright?"

It's not much, but I'll take it.

"Thank you." I nod again, and then I look around. "I'll see you tomorrow, then."

This time, I walk away, but I feel much better, almost lighter somehow. I don't even feel like I need a cigarette any longer.

When I arrived in town, I hadn't known the real reason I'd come; but as I make my way back toward Fairmont's one decent hotel, I have a feeling I at least had something worth coming back for: A new chance.

Once more, I see Martha's bright smile as she passes me her peach pie; I see her laughing on our wedding day; I see the twinkle in her eye as she tells me she's pregnant for the first time.

Then I left, and then I was gone.

The past is gone.

And now she's gone, too.

But the future no longer looks quite the same as it did before I came, either.

I see Asher marrying his girlfriend; I see Matthias standing around, pretending not to care he's home; I even see Sama, baking in Martha's old kitchen.

And perhaps I even see myself, not a favorite visitor, but a visitor nonetheless.

It is a small hope, but it's more than I deserve.

PEACH GLAZE PIE

AN ENGLAND FAMILY RECIPE

From the kitchen of Jane Rogers England, shared by her daughter Brittany

PEACH GLAZE PIE

Ingredients:

6 medium peaches

1 TBSP lemon juice

¼ cup sugar

3 TBSP cornstarch

2 TBSP butter

½ TSP salt

1/8 TSP almond extract

¼ cup sugar

Baked pie crust

Directions:

Peel and slice peaches. Add lemon juice and sugar and allow to set overnight.

Drain peaches, reserving syrup.

Add water to syrup until it makes 1 cup.

Sift together sugar and cornstarch; gradually add syrup and bring to a boil, stirring

constantly.

Cook 3 minutes, or until mixture is clear.

Remove from heat and add salt, butter, and almond extract; mix well.

Add peaches and mix gently.

Put filling into baked pie crust and serve with

whipped cream or ice cream.

JANE ROGERS ENGLAND, SHARED BY HER DAUGHTER, BRITTANY ENGLAND BURDEN

"My mom was always humming her own tune in the kitchen. She loved music and food, I guess because those are two things you can fully give yourself over to. She wanted to live big, and she experienced those things through her food and music."

TELL NO PIES

A HUSBAND MINCES HIS WORDS

Life of Pies, Book 11

C. S. Johnson

CHAPTER ELEVEN
Donnie Hennessey

It doesn't matter how long Edith and I have been married, she still insists on dragging me out to do things I never, ever want to do.

And I never, ever want to go to the Fairmont Spring Festival.

"Donnie, are you coming?"

I grimace at her voice.

She sounds so damn cheerful, it makes me want to shoot myself.

Hell, I do want to shoot myself—it's not like I haven't done it before.

My hands clench at the memory.

But this time, I'd make sure the damn gun doesn't misfire.

"The pie contest is coming up, and I want to be there for the judging," Edith says. Even though she's in the next room, I know she's finished cleaning up the kitchen, and she's now searching for her purse.

I grit my teeth as pain shoots up my back. I struggle to stand up, but I do my best to hide it. If I can hide it from others, I like to think I can hide it from myself.

It's stupid to think it, but I still think it.

I shake my leg a little, working out the tingles.

It doesn't matter how long it's been; I can still feel the shrapnel hitting my right side, splattering into my skin and burrowing into my flesh.

My teeth start to hurt as I grind them together in my mouth.

Everyone says I'm a hero, but I certainly don't feel heroic, no matter what my Purple Heart badge implies.

"Hun? Are you ready?" Edith calls from the other room.

My patience snaps. "You know well enough I don't want to go, Edith, so be grateful I'm getting up, even if it's a bit slow for you."

"Come on, Donnie, Martha's pie—"

"Yeah, yeah, I know," I grumble. "I also know Martha's dead, and her corpse isn't going to give a damn if she wins, either."

"Donnie." Edith appears at the door. Right away, I notice she's put on earrings and even some make-up, and she's wearing one of her nicer dresses and the pearls I'd given her for our first anniversary. She seems so much … *younger.*

And I won't say that aloud; but she frowns at me, as if she heard me say it anyway.

Back when we were dating, I would've said she was pretty.

I don't say so now—after all, we're married; I figure she ought to know she looks pretty on her own.

Why else would she do it?

"This is important to me," she practically whimpers.

"Why? It's not like it's *your* pie." I grab my cane and roll my eyes. I hate her sad eyes. Several years of dealing with widows and enemy spies—plenty of whom were willing to use sad eyes to get their way—have ruined me, and Edith ought to have figured that out by now. "God knows a pie you make wouldn't last a full minute against one from Orpah or Martha."

Edith fumbles with her dress, and I know I've made her upset.

I don't mean to, but she's so unrealistic about things sometimes.

I can glance around the room and see her real estate yard signs, her make-up kits, her essential oils, and even a couple jars of vitamin shakes she'd been selling over a decade ago. Edith keeps her failures all around her.

I catch sight of myself in the mirror. My back is erect with militaristic pride, and my outfit seems uncharacteristically loose on me. The jacket is unnecessary but I've worn it as a habit, and I don't feel like breaking it; my hair is crinkly and white, my skin looks almost gray, and my skin tags and liver spots make me feel like some kind of goddamned cartoon villain taking a vacation.

Ever so slightly, I slump forward; I ought to be glad Edith's failures include me, I guess.

"Well, it's still important to Clarice, and Sama, and Judge Piper, too," Edith says.

She probably thinks adding the judge into the list will impress me, but even though I respect the man, it doesn't make me move any faster.

She sighs, seeing my apathy. "This is for Martha's legacy, Don."

"I don't care."

And that's the honest to God truth.

I *don't* care.

I care that every movement I make, I feel more pain, and I'm just expected to deal with it. No one else has to deal with it, so I have to.

No one else has to deal with my past, either. It's more painful than my knees and back and arms, and all the other issues with my body.

All the images of the past seem to haunt me purposefully, as if the brightness of today just has to be ruined with images of dead children lying on the street, men bleeding out from having their organs harvested, women weeping as they're raped, a

traitor using my family to threaten me … fires breaking out, missiles flashing overhead, the last planes taking off …

Quietly, I push those thoughts away.

I'd served proudly, knowing I'd do a job that not everyone could. But since I'd been discharged, the battlefield only came back with me, and I have to repeatedly remind myself of that.

I know it's not fair, but life isn't fair.

I've made enough stupid decisions over the years to know I'm probably better off than I think I am.

Even if that means I have to go to the goddamn pie contest.

Edith licks her lips, imploringly and impatiently. "You promised me that you would go with me," she reminds me.

"Fine." I wave at her dismissively. "Just get in the car, would you? I'll get the keys."

She smiles, holding them up in her hand. "Already got them."

"Fine," I say again.

We walk out to the car in silence, but I'm tempted to grumble and complain and even yell at Edith.

The pain in my knees and back screams at me through each turn and quick stop—doesn't matter how many years I've been out of the military, I still drive like a demon's at my heels. It's to Edith's credit that she lets me drive at all.

We don't say anything as we drive; I'd rather complain, but I know I'm already on Edith's nerves.

And if I am honest with myself, complaining doesn't help. It's an outlet, and a desperate one.

My knee twinges as I pull into the festival and I almost hiss in surprise pain. My hands tighten around the steering wheel.

"Oh, look!" Edith says cheerfully. "The Robinsons have their custom wind chimes for sale again. I've been meaning to get some."

I grunt out a nonsensical reply.

"And there's the McKinley's petting zoo," she says, pointing eagerly. "Maybe if we find Sama, I'll take her over there. She likes animals."

"Just make sure she's not allowed to hold them. No one needs to watch an animal die while we're here," I mutter.

A few years ago, Edith told me Sama had thrown a small feral kitten after it'd bitten her. Martha wasn't happy with that, and I hadn't been, either. The kitten had hit my window and I'd practically launched myself off the couch at the noise.

Edith sighs. "Oh, Donnie, that's not nice to say."

"What?" I roll my eyes as I turn into an empty parking spot. "You know as well as I do that kid doesn't need to be near any animals."

"It's still not nice. You'll hurt Sama's feelings if she hears you."

"I doubt she'll hear me in my own car."

I hate how people just pretend Martha's kid is not retarded—it's like how they just ignore me and my injuries.

Regular people don't do us any favors when they pretend not to notice. They're doing *themselves* a favor, so they don't have to face the uncomfortable truths about life. They can pretend we're all hunky-dory and skip over feeling sorry for us by feeling good about themselves.

It's all so unbearably smug and self-congratulatory.

A few moments pass in silence as I turn off the car, climb out, and start walking. Edith smiles and waves to people she knows as we walk. I just ignore them; that makes them happier, and it makes me happier, too.

"Promise me you'll be nice in front of our neighbors. Sama and her family have had enough trouble lately."

I give her a sidelong glance. "I'll be nice—if you don't smoke."

Edith bristles, and I feel better.

From the expression on her face, I know she'd love another cigarette, but I'm tired of the smell as much as the cost.

I also hate how Edith coughs at times; I've noticed it more in the last few weeks, but she's content to chalk it up to allergies and the pollen and such.

Honestly, I'd respect her more if she was genuinely suicidal, rather than eager to die by a thousand carcinogenic inhales.

"Would you like to go the Veterans booth?" Edith asks me.

Sometimes, she's just as bad as the rest of them, I think glumly. She knows I don't want to be here, and I don't want to have a good time, and I don't want to see anyone.

My jaw tightens as I force myself to be polite. "No."

I see the other guys regularly enough as we're waiting down at the VA, trying to get refills on our meds, but I don't tell that to Edith.

She lives in a world of illusions, and as much as they irritate me, I do still want her to be happy. I just know I can't do that for her.

I couldn't give her children to do it for her either.

Thankfully, she's distracted by the crowds, and especially eager to get to the pie contest—which, of course, is all the way in the back of the fairgrounds.

It's like the devil knew I'd be coming, so he had the planning committee make it as inconvenient as possible for me to get back there.

"I wonder what's going on?"

Edith's surprised tone makes me look up. In the distance, I can see there's a police car inching its way out of the festival grounds. Its lights are on, and even through the darkened glass, I can see Orpah Abraham's large, ruby-red lips moving in outrage.

I almost laugh. Orpah's the biggest, phoniest phony ever, and whether it's politics, TV, or fashion, she has the stupidest people following her.

I wonder if Solomon McCain is questioning himself over his own infatuation with her. It's hard not to laugh at his expense, especially when I notice his grim look as he slowly drives past us.

I've never liked him much either, so seeing him depressed as hell is funny to me.

"I wonder if he'll get rid of his signed portraits of her that he has in his office," I mutter.

"I wonder what happened," Edith says. "Surely he's not actually arresting her? Ooh, I knew we should've left earlier. We missed everything!"

"If they've announced the pie contest winner, I want to leave," I tell her, but she's still caught up in her happy musings.

"Do you think she hit someone?" Edith asks with a surprise giggle. "I'd love that. I know Pamela and Matthias came here earlier with Sama. Maybe she confronted Judge Piper!"

"Don't worry." I nod toward the crowd up ahead. "You'll get the gossip here shortly."

Just then, Clarice Youngblood, Edith's other best friend, calls out to us and waves.

Edith perks up, but I don't alter my pace at all. I'll hear the official story on the news, if Orpah doesn't manage to get the story shut down before then. I've seen some of her fancy New York lawyers in action before; I doubt it'll get far. Even if her lawyers can't stop it, she'll get some of her famous friends to step in to support her, or she'll get some sympathic young'uns to start a legal fund, or even some of her reporter friends will try to bury the story or change it so it's someone else's fault.

I'm old enough to know the playbook by now, and I'm smart enough to ignore it. My own peace of mind is more important.

"It's Martha's pie!"

Clarice's shrieking slices through my distracted thoughts. A second later, I watch as she runs up to Edith.

She takes my wife's hands in hers. If they'd've been forty years younger, or even thirty, Clarice would've been jumping up and down. "Edith, did you hear? Martha's pie won!"

"It won?" Edith's eyes fill will tears, and Clarice hugs her.

What is wrong with you two?

It's a pie, for God's sake.

I ignore Edith as she runs toward the head of the table where they're handing out ribbons to the runner-ups. Mayor Bottoms is in his prime as he goes around preening, and the local press goes around taking pictures and asking for quotes. I'd say it was re-election season for him, but for a politician, it's always re-election season.

Others start to gather around, too; now that the judging is over, more of the crowd is moving in for samples, and some will buy a slice for later.

I head over to the table as the crowds disperse. I can head Clyde Montgomery buying the rest of his wife's plum pie as she sobs quietly off to the far side.

Must be nice to have money.

I imagine it's easier to be a failure when you have money.

I look down at the table and watch as the rest of the slices are methodically packed up and taken away. I hear a few people asking for Orpah's pie, and I almost laugh as the volunteer workers turn them away, and another lady says it might be poisoned from the sound of it.

Orpah's fame is already turning into infamy.

Now, there's only one pie left that remains untouched.

I look down and see it's a mincemeat pie—whatever the hell that is.

The judges for the contest only took a small slice, and then they'd left the rest behind.

I just watch the pie as Edith and Clarice talk with the local paper and the mayor.

Edith's happy.

"This is a great day," she says. "I only wish Martha was here to see it."

"Ma'am, is there any truth to the gossip that says Orpah didn't use her own pies for the last twelve years?" the young girl journalist asks.

Clarice huffs. "Her assistant confirmed that she had to go all the way down to the Fresh Market Village for her pie this year. Do you really think it was any different before?"

"But is there proof?"

"I'd only like to go on record saying that it's a shame such deception will forever plague our community," Clarice continues primly.

I cross my arms and lean back against the table, watching her. If she wants, Clarice could give the mayor a good run for his money—especially if he goes too soft on Orpah's pie scandal.

Which he probably will, unless she's convicted; Orpah's given the mayor money for his campaigns before. It's not exactly a secret.

"I'm just glad the truth was discovered," Edith stammers. "Next year, we may have to rethink some of the pie contest requirements, but it's still better that the truth came to light."

William Shakespeare, my wife is not.

I'm more than a little embarrassed for her.

"Excuse me, sir?"

A volunteer taps my shoulder. She's another young lady, probably one of the few newer young people who married into the townsfolk recently.

"What is it?" I ask, decidedly not eager for this conversation.

"Were you wanting to buy a slice?" She nods toward the mincemeat pie. "You're standing in front of it."

"I'm waiting on my wife," I explain, nodding to where Edith and Clarice are now talking to Martha's family and Judge Piper. I see Garland Morris is there too, probably trying to beg Judge Piper to be let off the hook for some bet they'd made earlier.

"Oh. Well, would you want to buy it for her, maybe?" The young lady blushes, and I realize she's just trying to get rid of the pie before she has to throw it away.

I'm about to tell her no when I see there's something vulnerable and soft about her gaze as she looks at me.

Women, all the same.

"This is your pie, isn't it?" I ask, realizing what she is *really* asking for.

"Yes." She admits it without pride, and then gives me a bitter smile. "Jimmy and I are visiting his mom here for a bit, and he wanted me to enter. I told him no one would want my cooking."

I glance over at Clyde Montgomery, whose wife is looking up at him with stars in her eyes. They're older than ancient, it seems, the two of them, but there's something timeless between them.

"I'll buy it," I tell the lady. I pull out a twenty and hand it to her. "Here. Let me keep the pan, huh?"

The young lady seems stricken. "Are you sure?" she asks, as if she'd reconsider.

"Yeah, I gave the money, right?" I snatch the pie up off the table and look down at it. "What the hell's in mincemeat, anyway?"

"It's got some beef, and some nuts, and some fruit, and some spices," the lady says.

"Well, no wonder you lost," I snort. "There's too much going on in there for it to be good enough for these folks. Not when Diabetes is rampant in these parts."

The lady giggles, all while I'm stuck with an awful, last-place pie.

But she seems happier, and it hits me that she reminds me a little of Edith when we were younger.

No wonder I'd gotten suckered into buying a loser pie.

"Donnie?"

I turn around to see Edith waiting for me.

"What's that?" she asks, and I can tell by her tone she's not pleased.

"Here," I say, handing her the pie. "I got this for you."

Her lips are pursed, and I know I've annoyed her.

Good. I'm annoyed, too. Time to go home.

"You didn't want to buy any of Martha's pie?" Edith asks.

"No." I don't tell her I didn't want to buy the mincemeat one, either, but then she'd probably just get even more angry.

"But it's Martha's last pie."

"*I don't care*, Edith. Can we go home now?"

Edith looks sad for a moment, and then she sighs. "Yes."

We walk through the festival again, stopping every once in a while so Edith can talk with someone else. The mincemeat pie in her hands gets a few odd looks, but no one says anything about it.

We drive home and I can smell the mincemeat pie a little better. It actually smells good.

"Sama's doing better today," Edith says, trying to chat a little with me.

I don't like it, but I don't stop her.

"She says Pama's been good to her."

"Who's Pama?" I frown.

"Asher's girlfriend," Edith says. "That's what Sama is calling her. Isn't that so sweet? I think he'll propose soon."

"I doubt it. Not until after his mother's funeral," I speculate.

"I think Martha would like that," Edith says. "I showed him where she'd kept her ring for him to use the other day."

"Uh-huh."

Edith continues to tell me about the festival, and Martha this, and Martha that, and how she'd love to see Orpah go to jail, and how Judge Piper wasn't that sad to be disqualified from judging, and how even Joe Davidson will be at the funeral with us tomorrow.

"Tomorrow?" I'm thankful we're nearly home as I turn to look at Edith. "The funeral is tomorrow?"

"Yes, and we need to go," Edith says firmly, already expecting my objection. "Martha's been our neighbor for years now and it's sad she's passed."

I groan as I pull in the driveway and turn off the car. "She's passed, and I'll be next at this rate, thanks to all your pushing me around."

"Well, then I guess it's good I'm such a failure about things, huh?" Edith snips back at me, and it's at that moment I realize she's actually quite upset. "If I didn't just fail all the time with everything, you'd be dead."

My knee stings, almost in warning, and I notice that she's clutching the mincemeat pie in her hands.

"Are you really upset about me buying a pie?" I ask. "It's my money, Edith. I'm allowed to buy what I like."

"You've never had mincemeat pie," Edith reminds me as she thrusts the pie pan into my lap. "You don't even know if you like it. And this one had the lowest score of the whole competition! It's not Martha's pie, that's for sure."

"Who cares about Martha's pie?" I watch as she gets out of the car in a huff, thanking God all over again I'm not a woman.

"Her pie won, though," Edith says. Her voice is half-muffled as she stomps away from me.

I limp inside with my pie in my hands, staggering pain still in my knee. "So? It's just a lemon meringue pie. Maybe I thought I'd like this one better. It's got all kinds of meat and nuts and stuff in it."

She crosses her arms and wrinkles her nose, and I'm suddenly very tired.

I'm tired of my pain, of having to explain myself, of just being awake. It's time for me to sit down, and I practically shove the pie on the counter.

"Not everyone gets to be a winner, Edith," I say, already heading for my recliner. "I know your pies wouldn't have won if you'd entered the contest, either, but I still eat them here when you attempt to make one. Just because you fail at things doesn't mean you don't have value."

Edith scowls at me, and I suddenly change my mind about the pie.

Turning around, I reach for a fork and pick up the pan. "It also doesn't mean I can't get a prize."

I take a bite out of the pie as she watches. It's nutty and meaty and spicy, that's for sure. There are too many things about it that pull on me, but for some reason, I think I like it, and I tell her so.

"See? I don't need a winning pie," I say. "I just need one I like."

She looks down at the floor. "Whatever, Donnie. I'm going to bed."

And with that, I head to my recliner, and she goes upstairs. Probably to pout, but who really knows?

I don't know how much time passes, but I do know after a few news broadcasts and some channel-swapping between sports highlights, I'm down nearly half the pie when the doorbell rings.

"Edith, someone's at the door," I yell, but there's no answer. I turn up the volume on the TV as the bell rings again.

I cock my ear as I hear Edith on the stairs. "Coming," she says.

"It's about time!" I holler. "And put on a sweater, would you? None of our neighbors want to see you in your old nightgown."

She mutters something I can't hear. Reluctantly, I turn down the volume again. I can hear Edith grab onto something, and I'm willing to bet it's her cigarettes. "What?"

"Nothing," she calls back before she opens the door. "Hi, Asher."

Oh, great. Martha's kid is back.

"Hi, Mrs. Hennessey," he says as she opens the door. "Sama is a little upset at the moment, and I was wondering if you could help me?"

"Sure, honey," Edith replies. "What's wrong?"

"Sama's finishing up her apple tarts from earlier," Asher explains. "But she can't find Mama's recipe book. Would you come over and help us look? I thought maybe you'd know where Mama might've placed it, and even if you don't, Pamela's a little busy with Sama's tantrum … "

I'm about to tell Edith to shut the door when he says, "Oh, wait. Is that it?"

I glance behind me, watching as Asher comes into our house. I see him stop at the counter, looking over a pile of Edith's stuff.

"I remember this," he says, pulling out a large, ugly-looking scrapbook. "Mama's stuff is all in here."

"Oh, yes," Edith says. "I borrowed it earlier this week. I'm sorry; I just plum forgot about it."

Earlier this week?

Edith never bothered Martha about her recipes—not that I knew of, anyway.

"Do you still need it?" Asher asks.

"No," Edith says, hurrying Asher back toward the exit. "Please take it back with my blessing. I won't be cooking anything new this week after all."

A new idea forms in my mind.

Edith with Martha's recipes? Martha's pie won at the festival …

I look back at my wife as she shuts the door, whirls around, and heads back upstairs. She deliberately ignores me.

And that's it.

She leaves me to my own devices and heads back to bed.

She doesn't want to tell me that she—or Clarice, maybe—made Martha's pie at the contest. She doesn't want to tell me that she is the real winner, and that I was wrong about her, and maybe that I was wrong about us.

With nothing else to do, or say, or prove, I shrug. I turn back to my mincemeat pie and take another bite.

And it's good enough for me.

OLD-FASHIONED MINCEMEAT PIE

A BAILEY FAMILY RECIPE

From the kitchens of Kay Henson Cole and her Grandmother Bailey

OLD-FASHIONED MINCEMEAT PIE

Ingredients:

2 9-inch pie shells

3 cups mincemeat (28-30 oz jar)

1 ½ cups chopped apples

Directions:

Mix mincemeat and apples together and pour into one pie shell. Cover with the second pie shell and cut slits in the top.

Bake at 425° for 40-45 minutes, until crust is nicely browned. Serve slightly warm.

"When I first started working on this little cookbook, I had to agree with Donnie Hennessey (Life of Pies Chapter 11: Tell No Pies): What on earth is a mincemeat pie?

"After a bit of research, I learned a thing or two. First, I learned that mincemeat pie – sometimes simply called mince pie, or even Christmas pie – is an old-world pie that used to be served, not as dessert, but as a hearty main course. I also learned that it has a religious history, with origins dating back to the Crusaders bringing home oriental spices from their travels, including nutmeg, clove, and cinnamon. Those three spices, when added to the mincemeat, represented the gifts of the three Magi to the Christ Child, with the pie shell representing the manger.

"Now that I knew what a mincemeat pie was, the hard part was finding someone who still makes them – or at least remembers a grandparent making them.

"I'm proud to say that my mission was completed when Kay Henson Cole, a friend of my mother-in-law, shared her grandmother's mincemeat pie recipe with me.

"My Grandmother Bailey was a terrific cook and I recall trying this pie as a child."

PRETTY PIES

Life Goes On for the Living

Life of Pies, Book 12

C. S. Johnson

CHAPTER TWELVE
Samantha Davidson

My mama is dead.

I can't think the words without crying.

I just want to cry.

I just want to cry and hit things.

I don't like the pain, but I know what it is. That helps and it hurts.

"Sama?"

My brother Asher knocks on my bedroom door and then peeks inside. I glance over at him from my spot on the floor.

My brother is so handsome. He has such pretty blue eyes and blonde hair, and he has a very nice smile.

I have missed him so much. He went to live in Georgia to go to college for his business degree. Mama was always proud of him. I was, too. But I missed him.

I am glad to see him again.

He comes into my room, reaches down, and offers me his hand. "Let's get going," he says. "It's time for the funeral."

I pull back. I don't really want to go.

"Mama's dead, Asher," I say, and he nods.

"I know, Sama." He pulls me up off the floor this time in a quick, playful way. Even though I'm sad, I smile.

I do love my brother.

"Come on," he says. "Pama is waiting for us in my rental car. She's packed up your apple tarts for the funeral."

I cheer up a little. Pama is Asher's girlfriend, and she is very pretty, too. She seems like a good match for my brother. She is very smart and kind, too. I liked making apple tarts with her yesterday after we came home from the festival.

I like baking. Mama and I did it together a lot, and I enjoy having Pama's company. I smile at the thought of her trying to crack eggs; I could tell she hadn't done it in a long time, if she'd ever even done it at all, and I showed her how to do it the way Mama taught me.

"I think Mama would've liked Pama," I tell Asher quietly. "She's very nice."

Asher nods. "I think she can be."

"Are you going to marry her?" I ask. I am glad we can talk about something else. And as much as I miss Mama, I think a wedding would be much happier.

"Maybe," Asher says. He looks hesitant, so I frown at him.

"Do you love her?" I ask.

He puts a finger on my nose playfully. "I love you," he tells me, and I hug him. "I don't know if Pama would want to move out here to help me take care of you. She and I both have to finish school, and then we'd have to find new jobs. I'm not sure she'd be able to get a job in Fairmont. I'm not sure she'd agree to marry me if we couldn't figure that part out."

"Why not?" I ask. "She loves you, too, right?"

"Yes. But sometimes love isn't enough to make commitment work." Asher shrugs. "But don't worry about us. Not right now, at least. We've got to get to the funeral.

"Pip will be there," I say, brightening up.

"Yes, and speaking of Pip, he called me this morning and told me he got you a corsage for the funeral, so don't wear too much jewelry."

I hold up my arms, showing him my collection of bracelets. "Too late!"

He laughs and I laugh with him, and he gives me another hug.

Asher's always been a good brother to me. He takes my hand and leads me out of the house. In the driveway, I can see Pama sitting in Asher's car. Beside them, Matthias' car is there, and he's standing beside it. Like Asher, he is wearing a suit, but he doesn't seem happy or sad. He looks more sullen.

I don't think he likes me much. I haven't seen him much at all in my life, even though Mama would talk about him to me. She told me he had a big job in Nashville, and he had a mean boss who wouldn't let him leave. I told her once that we should go rescue him, and she laughed.

"Matthias wouldn't like that, as nice as it would be to see him," she said. "Matthias is a man, and he needs to figure out how to rescue himself. But don't worry. We'll keep praying for him to come home one day, and he will."

He didn't seem happy he was home. But then, Mama was dead, and he'd let his mean boss keep him from seeing her all these years. I would be upset, too.

Maybe I would be meaner, too. He may not like me too much, but Asher and Pama and Pip do, and so do others.

I see Miss Edith walking out of her house. She stands on her porch, wearing a black dress like me, and she's still wearing the same pearls she always wears. But she seems extra-pretty today, even though it's a sad day.

She pulls out a cigarette and lights it, and then waves to us. "We'll be heading to the funeral home soon," she promises. "Or at least, I will."

"Donnie doing okay?" Asher asks.

Edith gives him a half-smile. "He ate so much of his mincemeat pie last night, he's got stomach pains this morning. I don't think he'll make it, but I'll be there, and I'll be able to set up for the food afterward."

"Oh, that'll be great," Asher agrees. "Thank you."

"What food?" I ask as I get into the car and buckle. Mama always told me to buckle when I got into the car.

"After the funeral takes place, a lot of times people will eat together," Asher explains as he starts the car.

"That's right," Pama agrees. "It's a way for people to share their grief together and comfort each other. And it's a way to make sure the deceased's family has some food while they mourn. Sometimes when people are really sad, they forget to eat."

She hands me back the Tupperware container full of my apple tarts. "I'm sure everyone will love these."

"We know you do." Asher takes her hand and kisses the back of it like a gentleman. "You ate three of them last night."

Pama's nose twitches, but she nods. "You've always known I like them, Asher," she mumbles.

I think she's embarrassed, but she lets Asher keep hold of her hand as we drive to the funeral home.

Twelve Oaks Funeral Home is a very nice-looking place. I don't like that we have to go there, because it's Mama's funeral, but at least it looks nice. It smells kind of funny, though.

Asher and Pama walk with me through the gathering room, and that's when I see Mama.

A funeral director lady comes up to greet us, and as she's talking with Asher and Pama about the food we'll be having after the funeral, I slip away from them to go see Mama.

I walk up to her coffin. It's got a lot of cushions in it. I am glad for that. I don't think she looks very peaceful. Her eyes are closed and her skin seems strained, as if it's pulled back from her face somehow. Her hair is more silver than blonde as I look at it. Her hands are folded in a nice way together on top of her stomach. She's wearing a blue dress.

Mama liked blue. She said it went well with her eyes.

I often wish I'd gotten more of Mama's looks. She has such pale skin and light coloring. I'm more tan and dark, and my hair is black, too, with some tighter curls.

I don't remember my daddy, but that's why I like Pip so much. It's much easier for me to pretend he's my daddy.

Mama told me that Matthias and Asher have a different daddy, and he left them. She says she couldn't blame him, but it was hard not to hate him sometimes since it meant we didn't have a lot of money and she didn't have a lot of help with all of us.

It didn't help at times that Orpah Abraham would come along and threaten Mama. They never liked each other much.

I am glad Orpah was arrested.

I don't think she is in jail anymore, though. Her lawyer got a counter-suit up, or so Matthias had mentioned earlier. He also said she is out on a cash bail. I'd heard Asher say if she knew what was good for her, she'd leave me alone.

I agree with him. I don't want her to bother me.

I don't want her at the funeral.

I can still see her mixing that powder into Mama's gravy. I didn't want to say anything because I didn't want her to kill me, too.

But then Matthias came home, and Mama ate with him while I'd been crying softly in my room.

I'd let Mama die.

I take hold of her hand. "I'm sorry, Mama. This is all my fault."

I put my head on her stomach and cry. My nose runs and my head aches and my whole body feels warm as I stand there.

I just want my Mama.

Mama would embrace me and pull me close and I would be able to smell her and hear her heartbeat. Sometimes I would push her away because she crowded herself into me.

But now I can't feel her, smell her, or hear her. God already took her up to Heaven, and he left the body behind.

For a long time, Mama and Asher were my only family. When Asher left, it really was just me and Mama. Sometimes Pip, too, but Mama was always there for me.

And now she's gone.

I cry harder.

There are some shuffling noises behind me, and I look up briefly, only to see an old man behind me. He's wearing a suit, too, but it doesn't seem to fit him. He has dark blonde hair like Mama's but it's more gray in the back.

I don't know who he is.

Before I can go back to crying, Pama comes up from the other side and tugs my arm. "Hey, Sama," she says. Her voice is a little too light and sweet and she seems a little worried. "Asher asked me to take you into the back kitchen. There's a small room on the other side of the funeral home where we'll be eating, and he thought you'd be good at making sure the food is organized."

"Okay."

I wipe my running nose off on my arm. Pama winces and grabs a tissue from one of the many boxes placed around the funeral home.

"Here, let me get that," she says. There's a frown on her face, and I remember that people are grossed out by snot.

I clean my hands off with some sanitizer, and Pama does the same as we head into the kitchen.

Lots of food has come in. There's a full plate of turkey, with some ham, and bacon salad, ham salad, potato salad, and macaroni salad; there's also some fried okra, some string beans, and what looks like some jambalaya.

Ew. I hate jambalaya.

I glance behind me and see some rolls, bread slices, plenty of butter, a small salad bar, and then the dessert table.

In the middle of it is my pan of apple tarts.

I'm pleased to see them arranged so nicely.

Mama would've been proud.

I see Pama welcome Miss Edith to the kitchen, since she's arrived now. I start to check on the other food and rearrange some of it as they chitchat.

"Oh, you look lovely in that dress, Pamela," Edith says. "Asher's a real lucky man, isn't he?"

"I like to think so," Pama agrees. "He seems to think he is, too."

"Well, he is," Edith says. "I'm only sorry you didn't get to meet Martha yourself. She was a sweet lady."

"I'm sure she was. Sama, can you help me with this?"

I look over to see she's pulled out a large bowl of chili and put it on the stove.

"Where is the crockpot?" I ask. "It needs to go in there."

"Oh." Pama seems surprised, and then she blushes. "I don't know much about cooking," she tells Edith apologetically.

"That's why you got Sama and Asher," Edith replies as she pulls out the crockpot warmer from a bottom cupboard.

After a little while, more people come in, including the pastor from one of the local churches.

Mama didn't always like to take me to church, outside of Christmas and Easter, but she was a God-fearing woman.

At school, someone once told me that other people didn't like my mama because she was a white woman and dating a black man, and then there were some that didn't like her because she was divorced and dating another man, and then there were some people who said she just didn't want me to see all the other people's ugliness.

When I told Mama that, she told me some people didn't want to see her because of Matthias and Asher's daddy leaving them, and then later, they didn't like that she'd been Pip's girlfriend. They liked her well enough, but they didn't want her around much, and she didn't like it all the time, but she respected that.

That's just part of life, she'd told me. The world can only get better one person at a time, and you do your best to live in such a way that people walk away changed.

My mama was a very nice lady. She got mad at me before, and I'd been mad at her, too, but I know she loved me. And she loved Matthias and Asher, and her friends and Pip.

And I love them all, too.

The pastor talks with Edith most of all, and then Pama leaves me as she goes to get Asher and Matthias.

The music plays a little louder, but I'm content to stay where I'm at. The kitchen is a place where I felt at home, and since Mama died, I haven't felt much at home.

I toss the salad, I mix up some special dressing with the oil and spice I find in the cabinet, and I put some icing on the sugar cookies.

"You're busier than a little bumblebee in here, aren't you?"

"Pip!" I glance up to see Pip smiling at me. His eyes are sad but I still run over and hug him. He holds me close and pats my back in comforting circles.

"Will you sit with me through the service?" he asks.

I nod. "Okay."

I've never been to a funeral before. I sit down next to Pip, and Pama and Asher are on my other side. I see Matthias is standing in the back, but at least he looks less sullen and more sad now.

On the other side of the room, I notice the man I'd seen earlier. His fingers are clenching and unclenching at his side.

"Don't pay him any mind," Pip whispers beside me.

I turn around to face the front. "Who is that?" I ask, but before Pip can reply, the music stops, and the pastor steps up to the small podium off to the side of Mama's coffin.

The pastor gives us a nice service, talking nice about my Mama. He says she was a very loving woman and a good mother. He says she was also a good baker. I am ready to cry again as he closes in prayer.

When he finishes, he sighs.

"She was this town's true pie queen," the pastor says solemnly.

"That's right, she was," a voice calls out from the back.

Pip and I glance around and I see Memaw, the old lady who runs the Fresh Market store. Mama and I had seen her a few times over the years when we'd gone to visit, and Memaw always welcomed us. She'd talk with Mama about all kinds of pies.

More people are getting up and moving, and the pastor reminds everyone that there's food in the back room.

I am happy I helped set up, and I am about to take Pip's hand and lead him back there when Memaw comes up to me.

"Precious child," she whispers as she hugs me. "I'm sorry about your Mama. But if you ever want to bake with me again, you just give me a call, and I'll find a way to come up."

"I'm sure you have other responsibilities," Pip says a little coldly. "I'll be here for her."

Memaw gives him an assessing look. "Well, certainly I have much to do, but it can all be set aside for love," she says.

"Is that why Orpah Abraham trusted you to bake her the pie she tried to enter into the contest this year?" Pip asks, still a little harshly.

Memaw scowls. "My granddaughter is hardly my responsibility any longer, good sir. I didn't know about the pie fiasco, but I won't apologize for my baking, either.

It's part of the reason Martha was as good a pie maker as she was, thanks to my learning."

Pip says nothing as I hug Memaw again. "Thank you," I say.

"Maybe you can come and stay with me, too," Memaw says, her ancient smile both fun and frail.

She gives me a kiss on the forehead.

"I like her," I say to Pip. "She's always been very nice to me."

"Well, of course she would be," Pip whispers as he squeezes my hand. "She's your great-grandmother."

"She is?" I blink my eyes wide with wonder, watching as Memaw heads out of the room.

Pip doesn't say anything else, since Pama comes up to us.

"We've saved you some seats in the fellowship hall," she says as she takes my other hand. "Asher and Matthias are already there. Would you come and join us?"

I look back at Mama's coffin.

I'm still sad.

I still miss her.

I know I will cry about missing her for years to come.

But I tighten my hands around Pip's and Pama's.

I have some good apple tarts there to serve to other people.

We get to the reception and I watch as my apple tarts consistently disappear.

"Oh, these are great, Miss Samantha," Officer Solomon McCain says to me as he grabs the last one. "You've inherited your mother's great skills. Perhaps you'll be entering the pie contest next year?"

Miss Edith comes up beside me. "Oh, that would be lovely! Clarice and I can sponsor you! And Martha would be so proud. If that's what you want to do, I mean."

"You'll have my bet." Garland Morris smiles as he calls out to us. Matthias, standing next to him, just shrugs.

The older man in the not-fitting suit taps me on the shoulder. "Perhaps you can do even better than Martha," he suggests. "Plenty of the people here and other places would probably really love to buy your treats."

"Oh!" Asher puts his arm on the man's shoulder. "You mean she should open her own business?"

"Yes." The man nods at me and gives me a brilliant smile. "Martha had her catering business, after all. Perhaps you can open a bakery here. What do you think?"

It takes me a moment to think it over, but I'm already nodding. "That would be wonderful, sir."

"I think it's great, too, Papa," Asher says.

I frown at the man. Just then, I see the resemblance between him and Asher.

"You're Asher's dad?" I ask.

The man seems shocked by the question, but Asher nods. "Yes," he says. "This is Joe. Do you remember him, Sama?"

The room goes quiet.

I shake my head. "No."

"Well, Miss Sama … " Joe extends his hand to me, while Pip puts his hand on my shoulder behind me. "It's nice to be here today."

Pama gives him a small smile. "Yes. Thank you for coming."

Joe straightens. "I haven't always been there. But when you do happen to open your own store, I'll happily be your first customer. In fact … let me pay you now."

He reaches into his pocket and pulls out some twenties. He puts them in my hand, and then nods again.

"Thanks for letting me see Martha again, one last time," he says, and then he heads toward the exit. He reaches into his pocket and pulls out a box of cigarettes.

As he walks up to the door, he pauses by a trash can, and then he tosses his box away. It's still really quiet in the room, and I can hear the soft *thump* as the box hits the top of the trash pile.

"Wait." Matthias calls out to him, and that stops Joe from leaving.

The rest of us are still watching as my older brother goes up to him and looks him in the eye.

"Money doesn't fix something like this," Matthias snaps at Joe. "Why don't you stick around and actually work on helping out?"

"Help with what?" Joe askes.

He looks around, as if he's waiting for one of us to answer.

So I answer him. "My family."

I glance around, looking at all of them, grateful I can see them and show them off.

There's Asher, my big brother who's always loved me and looked after me; there's Pama, his bride-to-be, or at least, I hope so; there is Pip, who seems like a good dad to me; there is Miss Edith, and there was Memaw earlier, and Mama's friends and even Matthias.

Joe hesitates. "Look … this is hard. Money is just easier. Give me a call if you want. But keep the money, okay? It's not meant to be a bribe. Think of it as an investment."

He leaves then, and the rest of us just watch.

Finally, Asher speaks. "Are you going to leave, too, Matthias?"

Matthias watches his dad leave the parking lot before he turns back to us.

"Not yet, I guess," he says. "I better stay here and help Sama get her bakery started. What good is my background in marketing if I can't help my own family?"

My smile is so big it hurts. "Oh, thank you, Matthias!" I say, running over to hug him.

He lets me hug him, and he even politely holds me back for a quick moment.

Then he lets me go.

"Besides," he says, looking over at Mayor Bottoms, who is stuffing his face full of one of my apple tarts. "I don't want to leave until that God-awful sign with Orpah's face is taken down. Even if it's not true she murdered my mother, she's no pie queen. I think we can agree with that, right, Mr. Mayor?"

"Absolutely," the mayor agrees. Little crumbs spray out of his mouth as he swallowed quickly. "Maybe we can get a sign that says 'Home of Sama's Bakery?'"

"Sama's Sweets," I correct him, and he nods.

"It's a great idea," he says. "I will put it on my next re-election ticket!"

"Sama will need a location for her business, first," Pama says. "Would we be able to get some new equipment in Martha's old kitchen?"

"Oh!" Edith's eyes light up. "I know! I can find a place for her. I still have my realtor's license."

"You might want to wait a little while anyway. Sama still has to finish high school, remember? But when she's ready, I can help with the legal zoning," Pip offers, no doubt after seeing my pouty face. "Shouldn't be too hard to get an inspection done and some papers drawn up, right, Officer McCain?"

The policeman nods, and Morris rubs his hands together. "I'll be able to get a loan secured, too."

"And I can help with the finances," Asher offers. He glances over at Pama. "Maybe after I'm done with school."

Pama puts her arm through Asher's as she gives him a loving look. "I think that's a good idea. But we might need a bigger house, if you want me to come with you."

"I want you to come with him," I say, and the crowd around me laughs. "I'll make you some apple tarts."

Pama lets go of Asher and hugs me. "Well, that sounds like a good deal to me."

And then we're all hugging each other.

I feel good all of a sudden.

I just feel that way for a moment. Maybe not even a moment. A half-moment. But it feels good, and I am happy about that.

~

Later on in the evening, after the funeral, after we eat the food, and after Mama's burial, I step into the kitchen.

It's lonely in here. Pama and Asher are out for the evening; earlier, I saw Asher take Mama's ring out of her case.

Matthias is in his room. He's not happy about things, but he's been quiet. I think he's sad still, but I am, too.

I look around the kitchen and decide to bake.

I open the pantry, looking for what I need. I see a can of pumpkin on the shelf, and even though it's not fall, I decide it's for the best.

Mama loved pumpkin pies. She told me once that when she was pregnant with me, that's what she would crave.

"I miss you, Mama," I whisper, as I pull out the pie crust materials, and I start whipping up the pumpkin pie center.

The smell of the nutmeg and the cinnamon make me smile. I don't remember what Mama smelled like at the funeral anymore; I can feel her warmth, and I can remember that I have people who love me.

My mother is dead.

I will miss her.

I will look for her for the rest of my life; I will expect to see her and I will cry again when I see she is not there.

But she is still here. In a way. I miss her, but I love her, and because I miss her, my love for her will always be inside me.

While I miss her, I will work. I will keep going. I will carry her with me.

I will have my bakery, my family, my friends. My own business. I will have my dreams. And I will work to make them come true.

I put the pie in the oven and set the timer, and then I begin another one.

PUMPKIN CHIFFON PIE

A TAYLOR FAMILY RECIPE

From the kitchen of Gloria Amerson Taylor

PUMPKIN CHIFFON PIE

Ingredients:

½ cup firmly packed light brown sugar

½ TSP salt

½ TSP cinnamon

½ TSP nutmeg

¼ TSP ginger

¼ TSP cloves

¼ cup granulated sugar

2 eggs (room temp)

½ cup milk

½ cup heavy whipping cream

1 ¼ cups canned pumpkin

(not pumpkin pie mix)

Directions:

Combine first seven ingredients

Add eggs, milk, and pumpkin

Mix together

Add cold whipping cream and mix on high for 1 and 1/2 minutes.

Pour into premade pie shell

Bake at 350 degrees in preheated oven for 1 hour and 5 minutes. Do not open oven before

then.

Check pie. It should be puffed all across pie and

slightly jiggle. It will fall during cooling.

Serve cooled with whipped topping.

from
CRYSTAL MCGOUGH & GLORIA AMERSON TAYLOR

"Pumpkin pie is one of my favorite pies. I have a large family on my dad's side, and every Thanksgiving and Easter, we all gather together to celebrate. Second only to the sheer size of our family, the one thing that always stands out is the food.

My Aunt Gloria always brings a pumpkin pie – this is where my love of pumpkin pie stems from. Until recently, however, I didn't know there was a story behind the pie.

My dad passed away in an unexpected accident in 2013, when I was only 27 years old, so it is with a heavy, but also full heart that I share with you the story of my dad's favorite pie, in the words of my beautiful and loving aunt:

"I started dating my husband in 1971. I was an only child, with just my mom for family. He came from a family of seven children – he also had a mom and dad in there. He was the middle child, with three older and three younger siblings. I wanted his family every bit as much as I wanted him. We were married and shortly after that the family started getting together at his baby sister's house for Easter and Thanksgiving, sometimes hosting up to 90 people. Everybody is welcomed.

"One year I brought this pie, and it was a hit. My husband's baby brother declared that this was his favorite pie ever, and that I really must bring it every year. I have. Every time I make it, I think, 'This is Wade's favorite pie.' We lost that sweet brother in a motorcycle accident, but as long as I'm able, I'll make Wade's favorite pumpkin pie."

AUTHOR

C. S. Johnson is the award-winning, genre-hopping author of several novels, including The Order of the Crystal Daggers, The Starlight Chronicles, and The Divine Space Pirates series. With a gift for sarcasm and an apologetic heart, she currently lives in Atlanta with her family.

EDITOR

Crystal McGough is a journalist and editor who lives in Clay, Alabama. She graduated from the University of Alabama in 2010 with a degree in Journalism and Creative Writing. She is currently the editor for her local newspaper, The Trussville Tribune, where she has worked for the last 13 years. She is also a proud wife and homeschooling mother of four.

<u>IMAGES & PHOTOS</u>

All photos were legally obtained and are owned by their original owners respectively, with special permission given to use them in the publication of this book. AI generated photos are not currently subjected to copyright; they were created with the aid of GabbyAI, from the Gab.com platform, with the further use of free embellishing marks from Canva. There is no trademark and were used in accordance with US Fair Use laws.

AUTHOR ACKNOWLEDGEMENTS

My thanks to all of my individual recipe donors, and to my editor, Crystal, who generously went out of her way to find them.

Corrie Robert Lee Freeman Sibley was born in 1897 and died in 1974 in Fairfield, Alabama. She was the mother of Sarah Francis Sibley Ellis and grandmother of Letitia Ellis Taylor who contributed the blueberry pie recipe in this book.

Deborah Royster McGough is the mother-in-law of Life of Pies Cookbook co-author and editor Crystal McGough. Deb was a K-12 teacher for over 40 years and currently works for a small catering business in Trussville, Alabama.

Dale Sheehan is the daughter of Mary Banker and now a proud mother and grandmother, herself. She currently lives in Alabama with her husband Ed.

Alice Wright is a fun and adventurous mother of four who lives in Gallant, Alabama, with her husband Jesse and their children. Together, they run the Wright Family Sawmill.

Betty Duncan lived in Columbus, Mississippi, and married the love of her life at the age of 18. She first learned to cook after getting married, determined to be able to cook whatever her love wished for.

Sarah Francis Sibley Ellis was born in 1920 in Russellville, Alabama. Her daughter, Letitia Ellis Taylor, was born 1958 in Fairfield, Alabama, and is the proud mother of Crystal McGough, co-author and editor of the Life of Pies Cookbook.

Tabatha Feduska is a faithful Christian and mother of four who lives in Alabama with her husband and children. She loves crafts and cooking and is the ultimate homemaker.

Tascha Piatt lives in Irondale, Alabama, with her husband John and their four children. She and her daughters love to sew, cook, and craft together.

Kay Henson Cole is a proud mother and grandmother who lives with her husband in Oxford, Alabama.

Jane Rogers England was a loving mother and grandmother. She lived in Alabama and passed away in January 2022, surrounded by her family. Her daughter Brittany currently lives in Alabama with her husband Derrick and their two children.

Gloria Taylor is a proud mother, grandmother and aunt who lives in Louisiana with her husband Marshall. She has an amazing sense of humor and loves to make others laugh. Gloria is the aunt of Life of Pies Cookbook co-author and editor Crystal McGough.

Thank you for reading! Please leave a review for this book
and check for other books and updates!

www.ingramcontent.com/pod-product-compliance
Lightning Source LLC
Chambersburg PA
CBHW041151300726
48981CB00003B/222